Warning

This e-book contains sexually explicit scenes and adult language and may be considered offensive to some readers. This e-book is for sale to adults ONLY as defined by the laws of the country in which you made your purchase. Please store your files wisely where they cannot be accessed by under-aged readers.

Dedication

For Momma, it was always for you. I will miss you forever.

Aunt Effie, your inspiration for life and the ability to get up after every fall with that beautiful smile. Your laughter through the tears made the pain of losing her the best medicine. I love you.

Ralph Santolla, rest in peace Beautiful Soul. Your music will always inspire the words.

Je t'aime mon amour

My Husband Victor, the driving force to keep me moving. For giving me the opportunity to pursue my Dream, I love you always.

Chapter One

The swaying oak trees rustled the leaves that trickled down like raindrops hitting the ground. The humming calm of the morning breeze blew through the screen of the open window. Denise stretched her legs while yawning out loud, "Mercy." Awakening from a deep sleep, fading was the hypnotic dream of being in the arms of the Goddess. She could still feel her soft hand holding hers, walking under the shadows of the branches that covered the woods underneath the hazy clouds that tried to hide the bright moon. The shimmering rays of sunlight shining on her bed was a reminder of her reality. She was in the Florida woods at her sister's home. Continuing to stretch to get some motivation for the early morning hour, she sounded like a female feline who was in heat. All the whilst thinking to herself, "If I had to make a list of things most detested in my current living arrangements, these early morning awakenings topped the list."

Saturday Morning was supposed to be a day of rest, yet no soul in this house ever slept past seven. Grabbing the edge of the bed to lift herself up, she shuffled her feet around to find her slippers. Feeling the fluffy softness of the black feathers on the top of the slipper,

declaring, "There you are." Her legs felt fatigued standing up stretching. Catching a glimpse of herself in the mirror that hung above the dresser, Denise stared at the gray circles under her eyes. She frantically slipped her fingers around the lid of the mason jar fill with lotion sitting on the dresser. A concoction she had made up herself. It worked better than any skin cream on the market. Intensely rubbing the homemade miracle under her eyes, Denise suddenly stopped. She heard the nonstop boom of blaring melodies between the wall that separated the room from where the vocal one slept. The songstress was already singing at the top of her lungs this early hour. Snapping the girls voice box entered the mind as Denise continued to look in the mirror at herself.

"Oh, this morning life is killing me. Don't these imbeciles ever sleep?" She muttered.

Putting on her satin purple robe while opening the door, she made her way to the kitchen. The smell of the cooking pig also referred to as bacon consumed the home. All her nose cared about was the aroma of coffee. Strolling through the living room to proceed into the kitchen, she heard the troll whose voice was much deeper in the morning sarcastically greet her with his usual, "Hey Aunt Lezzy." Since

she is occupying his room, Hagen made the couch his bed. There was no avoiding him in the morning. She was happy he stayed more with the sperm donor rather than his mother. Her nephew, the troll gave her the nickname "Lezzy." She immensely resented it. A bird shitting on his auburn head of hair was the spell of the day. Giving the troll a sinister snarl, she trekked into the kitchen. The atmosphere changed to a peaceful calm with the softness of her sister Charlotte's welcoming voice greeting, "Good Morning Sis."

With one hand hovered over her eyes to dim the brightness of the sun radiating through the windows, and the other scratching her buttocks she recoiled. "What is good about this morning?"

Her sister sat at the dinette sipping on her coffee with a plate of pig and egg that she was about to feast upon. Denise glided toward the Mister coffee. The only mister she had any respect for, she poured his liquid magic into her cup. While listening to Charlotte's response to her question that was a tad so happy for this hour in the morning.

"Well, we woke up." Charlotte smiled.

"I would rather wake up in the darkness, greeting the moonlight while dancing naked in it."

"Is that what you do in those Piney Woods?"

"Why do you think the sisters hate me. I dance for the men then I get in my car buck naked. I drive straight to those woods in the buff to swirl amongst the trees like when I strip on my pole. The feeling of freedom consuming me." Denise expressed with exhilaration.

"Shush, Denise. Hagen is in the next room." Her sister whispered holding her index finger over her lips displaying a mischievous grin.

"Well you are the one who asked." Denise retorted raising her eyebrow.

Shifting her sapphire eyes up at Charlotte, she took a seat next to her sipping on her black magic brew.

"I don't know how you do these mornings. This is agony. Yet you do it with a big smile."

"It's called being a mom. I don't recall the last time I slept in. I guess I am used to it." She admitted. "And that I do have many things to be thankful for. I don't ever want to forget the blessings I have received."

Denise crossed her legs adjusting her robe. Sipping the coffee while flipping her long thick hair over her shoulder, "Are you about to give a sermon?"

"Geez no, who am I to be righteous? I am far from sermons. But I know that when I lost faith in him, he did not lose it in me. It's gotta say something for the Almighty."

"So, you are saying darkness invaded your heart?" Denise suggested.

Charlotte's disposition changed along with her voice.

"I know where this is going."

"Where is this going?" Denise glared wondering what was in her sister's thoughts. For some reason she couldn't read her sister's thoughts. Like the Angel, she was blocked.

Charlotte rubbed her fingers over Denise's hand. It made her suddenly flinch. The delicate touch aroused her inside. It had been weeks feeling the softness of a woman's hand. The luscious lips of a slippery tongue licking her mound. She didn't know how much longer she could go without release of the sexual tension bottled up inside her. She scooted away feeling the attraction for her own sister.

"I didn't mean to startle you." Charlotte sweetly smiled lifting her eyebrow up.

"I thought you were going to pull a Lucie on me. She is fixated about the tales of the curse. You know? The one supposedly bestowed upon our family. Every time I am around her she starts babbling. It's getting ridiculous. I don't believe in all the hocus pocus.

"So, you don't believe in the dark magic?" Denise curiously asked.

"Good grief no. I know you study that magic stuff. If that is what helps you find peace. I have nothing to say. It's different for me. I lost all faith. It restored itself, I guess. Analyzing real life is hard enough, why would one dramatize it more with silly beliefs?" Charlotte asked.

"To have something to talk about in this boring town I guess." Denise retorted.

"I'd rather watch soap operas."

Charlotte's quick response caused her to contract a serious case of the giggles, that Denise soon caught.

After regaining her composure, Denise couldn't take her eyes off the flames igniting in her sister's pupils. The vision made her giggle even more. The maleficent humor made her laugh out loud with her naïve sister joining in. Their moment was interrupted by her nephew, the troll joining them at the table.

"So, Lezzy you dance for men but like women? Isn't that a conflict of interests?" He boasted.

Leaning in towards Hagen with her lips puckered and ringlets of black curls covering her eyes, Denise sarcastically replied.

"You are absolutely right nephew. I use the bigots such as yourself."

Denise stood up from the table while giving a wink to the troll.

"Denise," Charlotte interrupted. "He is just a boy."

"Then he should go play with the little ones not patronize the wiser. If you play with matches, don't whine when you light the fire." She sardonically smirked.

Denise glared at Hagen sharing a moment of mutual disgust for each other. He took his stench off her to resume a conversation with his mother.

"That is where you are wrong Mom. I am a young man. Young but still a man. Being a youthful man, I don't get what a woman could do for another woman."

"And just what do you know about "doing"?" Charlotte curiously questioned.

"Well not much, but Dad has told me some things. You know I have been given the "talk." Hagen grinned.

Denise rolled her eyes while shifting the hair away from her face. She comfortably stood, leaning against the counter by the sink observing the conversation going on between the mother and son. Hagen was chauvinistic like his loathing father. Shaking her head at his shallow nature, she turned her head staring out the window. The view of Madeline sitting center of the oak tree with her legs stretched out along the branches caught her attention. The youngling had her notebook and pencil in hand. The girl appeared to be talking to someone. Attempting to zero her energy in on the girl, the connection was abruptly lost. A truck speeding into the driveway stirring the dust broke the channels. Mr. Charming himself got out waving at his daughter strutting towards the house. Denise counted to three in her head knowing his fist was about to start knocking at the door. She heard her sister yell, "C'mon on in."

The handsome disaster opened the door stomping the dust off his boots before hustling in.

"Ya ready Hagen?"

"That's right. It's family day for you guys." Charlotte smiled.

Denise huffed at the disgusting scene. How could Charlotte be so cordial to such a vile man? Her once abuser. Was this the forgiveness she had heard off? The restored faith her sister was guessing she had? She'd rather conjure up a spell. Inconvenience the bastard, or just out right make him miserable. That was much more delightful than this shit she was witnessing. Staying silent, she watched the family interact with the troll answering his father's question.

"Just about Dad. I just need to get my stuff together. My rod and reel with my tackle box are on the porch. I have to grab some extra clothes outta my room where Lezzy is staying."

The troll steering by her on the path to his room had the audacity to wink at her with a sleazy grin.

"Hagen, can you stop trying to antagonize your aunt." Charlotte scolded.

14

Denise could see the sincerity in her sister's eyes, turning towards her with an apologetic nod. Though sincere, Denise resented the notion that anyone needed to come to her defense. She could take care of herself. The troll was really starting to get on her nerves. It was lucky that he preferred to stay at the sperm donor's residence. His luck would be turning

very dark if she had to endure the remarks daily. Burning him at the stake was not enough for the horrid young but diseased mind. If it was up to her, he would be devoured by the horned one.

Norman scooted out a chair from the table sitting down to wait on his son. His stare upon her made Denise despise him more than his son. With apprehensive ravenous eyes, he watched her every move. She could hear his lustful thoughts. The energy conveyed this man wasn't getting any kind of sexual pleasure. Besides the lust he fantasized about, the energy also revealed he was wondering why she was still there? Sinking his stare more into her, he blurted out the question.

"How long are you going to bunk with Charlotte?" I would have thought you to be gone by now."

Before she could answer she heard naïve Charlotte annoyingly come to her defense again.

"She can stay as long as she wants too. Denise is family."
"Well she hasn't been around for years." Norman retorted.

"We are getting to know each other. Isn't that right, Sis?"

"That's right." Denise grinned agreeing while pouring another cup of coffee.

"I am happy you are getting to know each other. I really am but the fact is we don't really know her. I don't want to throw this in your face but, after Wendell, I have a hard time trusting any stranger to the family anymore. By the way is Madeline coming with me? I hoped she would."

Denise witnessed Charlotte assure Norman there was no trouble with their connection. The words if you can't trust family then who can you trust came barreling from Charlotte's ignorant mouth. The words were laughable. Did her sister forget about Sharon's betrayal? It made Denise get a little choked on her coffee knowing the truth. Her closed-minded sister wasn't aware the curse she did not believe in was influencing her current thoughts. The scenario made her want to explode in laughter but she kept her calm generating a smile at the two. Her sister got up from the table joining her

in front of the sink looking out the window. Charlotte turning to the sperm donor reported their daughter's activity.

"Madeline is currently in the oak tree having a conversation with nature. She has taken a notebook, pencil, along with a book to read. The water and crackers confirm she has her day planned. Fishing is not on the agenda today. I am sorry Norman, maybe next time."

"Yeah maybe next time." The man solemnly answered.

Denise dreaded to see the arrival of her nephew popping back in her surroundings. The only joy of his appearance was announcing he was ready to leave. He kissed his mother on the cheek exiting the home. Denise stared at the once couple talk about the children before saying their good byes. Flickering her fingers, she summoned a flock of black birds to hover over Norman's truck.

"See ya Lezzy. Oh, pardon me. I mean Denise. The boy says it so much, I guess it's stuck in my brain." Norman chuckled following his son out the door.

"Really? You have a brain?" she murmured to herself.

Denise continued to silently chant flicking her fingers. Her sister never noticed starting to gather the dishes off the table. Suddenly dropping the stacked dishes, sounds of hollering came from outside. Rushing to the window, Denise stared over her shoulder from behind. The sisters burst out laughing witnessing the flock of birds raining shit all over Norman, Hagen, and the truck. The sisters giggled hysterically hearing Norman yell, "Get in."

A cackling hurl came from Charlotte's throat admitting to her sister. "They deserved it calling you Lezzy."

"Yes, they did." Denise thought displaying a wicked grin.

Chapter Two

Madeline wrote in her book, lounged in the seat the tree was providing. The breeze picked up blowing her golden locks with a sudden jolt of light flickering through the branches. In a flash, the angel was sitting beside her. His presence brought a serene smile to her face. Beautiful as ever, he greeted her.

"Hello Madeline. I am very happy you have a quiet morning planned. Can I visit for a while?"

Madeline sat straight up with excitement of his presence. Her smiled turned into a sweet giggling grin.

"I would love that Sir Angel. Did Father give you the day off or something?" I did it again, didn't I? I greeted you with a question."

"Yes, you did Maiden. Not to worry, Gabriel is watching over things while I spend time with you." He smiled.

Her bright blue eyes couldn't resist another question staring into his gaze.

"Why are you calling me Maiden? And who is Gabriel?"

The angel held his sides in laughter. He finally composed himself smiling, "Here we go again. So many questions. Well I call you maiden because you won't quit referring to me as Sir. Call me by my given name, Michael. A maiden is a young woman or girl such as yourself who is not married. As for Gabriel, he is my brother. Your mother taught you about me and not my brother? A question now for you Maiden," He grinned.

Madeline shrugged her shoulders with a little smirk, "Well we are not catholic. I guess she teaches me what she knows."

Michael put his arm around her. "I guess she does." He smiled while pointing his finger up, "But you don't have to be catholic to believe in angels or know about them. It's amuses me how humans base their beliefs on religion. Religion will fool you, faith from the inner soul never does."

"Is that something you want me to remember?" she asked quietly.

"Yes, it is." Displaying a smile of amusement. "I see you have been writing. Can I read what you have written?"

Madeline's shyness emerged knowing he was about to read her words. Still, she handed him the book to read her personal but sincere thoughts that he was most likely already aware of. It was different with him. She trusted the angel with all her soul. Michael read her words aloud while she listened nervously, interlacing her fingers together.

"Humans are much like the beautiful trees we coexist with on God's earth. We start out as a seed that flourishes into a sprout. With plenty of care but, most of all love, the trees will grow into an exquisite beauty. Our lives much like the branches that grow on the tree take on their own special form. Though the branches are similar, they each travel their own paths. Some days the weight of the world is like the water-logged moss that covers the branches and we feel weak. We will fall like the leaves fall to the ground on some of our journeys. But even if the leaves shall fall during a season of life, it prepares us for the coming of new green leaves that will always bloom come next season."

The angel was silent for a moment. He knew Madeline was as pure as the words she wrote. The sophisticated writing for a young girl astonished him. Inside he thanked his Father for the creation of her. The analogy of the tree was beautiful. He began to speak of his own wisdoms.

"You are amazingly correct. A man's life resembles the trees. If only man would trust Father like the trees do. The days may be hot and dry, but with faith he will bring the rain to quench the thirst. He will lift up when all has fallen."

Looking directly into the angel's eyes she quoted, *"She is a tree of life to those who take hold of her. Happy are all who retain her. Proverbs Chapter Three, Verse Eighteen."* Madeline smiled.

"Very good. You have been reading Father's words. No soul is too young to be wise." Michael praised.

"I try to study every day. I need to find out answers. Maybe then I wouldn't ask you so many questions. I am in the search of the question that always lingers in my head. The question of why?" she confined.

The angel gave her a curious look, his facial expression spoke of his knowing but, unable to give her the answers. Before he could speak, she interrupted.

"I know the answers I seek you already know. I am not too young to be aware of this. It's the freewill you spoke to me about. I still must find the answers. I want to know why me? Why am I pure? I want to know why my family doesn't see it. The fire in my aunt's eyes. She bares the same fire as Wendell. I want to know why Beatrice is so captivated by it. I fear for my sister. Darkness dwells in the woods around us."

Michael closed the book of her writings he was still holding gripping it tightly. It was obvious to her, the angel knew. The despair showed in his face not being able to reveal to her.

"Madeline, I know you are frightened. I know of the fire in your aunt's eyes. I feel what is in your heart. It makes me ache all over. Do not be afraid child. I am here with you even when you cannot see me. I know you can feel me too. Call out to me in thought, or by mouth. I will always protect you. Fear no evil, for I am at your side."

The tears trickled like rain drops down her cheeks. Her voice became crackling with anxiety.

"I am afraid. Why can't it just be stopped. The bad man came after me. I knew he was mean from the fire that glowed in his eyes. My Aunt Denise is in hiding of her wicked ways. My momma is blind to it. She invited my aunt to stay here for as long as she desires. Nothing good will come of it. I fear Momma is blind to it."

The angel put his arms around her while shielding his magnificent wings around them. He then confessed, "There is evil amongst you child."

"What is it?" she asked trembling.

"Long ago, darkness was cast upon your family. It's wicked. Evil will try to come for you. You will know who they are, you will see the truth. I am here Madeline. You are protected."

Madeline lifted her head asking, "My family Michael. What about them?"

She watched the despair that entered the eyes of her best friend. Before he said the words she already knew.

"I can't protect them like I can you. Pray their free will brings them closer to the Father, the Son, and the Holy spirit. Those are the only things that can protect them. Their faith and obedience. It comes natural for you. Your soul was built that way. They must build their ladder to the heavens. They must kneel down to Christ, accepting the sacrifice of blood he gave for them."

"Did the son not die for me too? I must obey the same rules. I don't understand."

"Yes, Our Savior did sacrifice for all humanity. Sweet child, you were born to help the battle. That's all I can say. You are different. You can't be influenced by the darkness, sadly your family can." Michael explained.

"No Michael. Protect them, not me. Please I beg you. Don't let my family succumb to this evil." She begged.

The angel tightened his wings more secure around Madeline. Feeling his safe hold around her, she gave into her moment of sorrow while he comforted her from the harsh reality.

He lifted her sad face with his finger. The angel's soft gentle voice comforted her soul with truths.

"Madeline, one day you will have all the answers. I am here for you always."

Breaking his hold around her, the angel picked up the book beside her.
"Let's read for a while, your little mind shouldn't be consumed with so much. What is *Great Expectations* anyways?"

"A book by the author *Charles Dickens*. He is wonderful by the way." Madeline conveyed wiping away her tears.

"Oh, yes. Charles is wonderful. He creates his stories in the heavens now.
"Really?" she excitably asked."

The angel darted his eyes up in jocular motion.

"Yes, really. Now let us read. It will improve your vocabulary you long to strengthen. Even though, I think you are stronger with your words than you realize."

Madeline grinned with approval of his recognition. She sat up still in the arms of her friend. His glistening wings shielded around them. The rest of the morning she read her book to the angel with a few interruptions of questions she always had for him.

Chapter Three

Charlotte was putting the last few dishes from breakfast in the dishwasher. She thought about washing the few dishes by hand, but she felt an unusual case of lazy coming on. Walking from the table to the dishwasher, she could see out the window with the view of Madeline lost in her own world sitting in the tree. Seeing the shadow of a presence behind her, she turned feeling Denise pressing her chin on her shoulder.

"What do you suppose Madeline is doing all day in that tree?" her sister curiously asked.

"Madeline is my book worm. She is reading while writing her own words. She is my quiet child, but she has more thoughts going on than we are aware. I am sure she has created a whole new universe in that tree. One that she is comfortable belonging too."

Charlotte continued to tidy the kitchen talking to Denise when she noticed that her sister was strolling around looking uneasy. Denise's discontent in her own thoughts expressed a sadness upon her face.

"You okay?" Charlotte asked.

"Yeah. It is just the words you just spoke of when I asked about Madeline. It struck a nerve. I am aware of the feeling of not belonging. The longing for one soul to understand." She confessed.

"Is that why you are distant from the family? You feel like you don't belong?"

"I don't belong. That's why Momma sent me away. She knew it too. From a young age, I knew I wasn't attracted to males. The men that lingered around the house that Daddy supplied with moonshine didn't help the interpretation either."

Denise began to stutter with a sudden shake overtaking her body. She breathed in deeply confessing, "One of those disgusting males took me."

A lump formed in Charlotte's throat searching for the right words. She turned to her sister putting her hands on both sides of Denise's forearms while sitting with her at the dinette.

"I never knew. I am so very sorry." She apologized.

Denise anxiously stuttered words before she was able to confess the sin committed against her in sentences. It was unusual to see her show any kind of weakness. Charlotte remained quiet until the confession began.

"I will never forget that day. The puncture of my insides. The burn that came with the vile man sweating all over me until he imploded with the stench of his loins. Momma tore him off me. She beat him almost to death sending him away to never return. I thought Momma had come to my rescue, but I was wrong. She blamed me for luring the man. I never left, she sent me away. The home she sent me to was a woman who served your God. For a woman of faith, she was one of the cruelest. I ran from that awful place hiding in the woods. That's when she found me. The one who changed my life."

"Who did you meet?" Charlotte curiously asked.

"I met. I met a."

Denise suddenly started to stutter again unable to say the name. It seemed strange to Charlotte but being extremely upset her sister needed comfort. She slid the chair over closer, holding her. The room remained silent for a moment. Denise took control of her composure continuing to speak.

"I met a friend who taught me another way. The peace of the earth. To honor it, love it, and it will love you." She confided.

"That doesn't seem so dark. It sounds comforting, very loving. Why does everyone think it's dark? I don't understand?" Charlotte admitted.

"Because she taught me more than that. She taught me not to pray for it, but to make it happen."

"I understand, kinda like I was done with praying, so on my own I dealt with getting out of my brutal marriage."

"I don't worship God. Why would I want to be part of your God's universe that allowed such terrible things to happen to me? I turned my back on such nonsense and have never looked back. My way gives me freedom. It can you too. If you allow it."

Charlotte lifted her hand up caressing her sister's cheek. She felt overwhelming compassion knowing the feeling of a man taking you. Even though the man that took her innocence was her husband, Charlotte understood the brutality of the act. The two sisters gazed into each other eyes not saying a word.

Denise eased in closer to her. Her mind became foggy staring into her sister's eyes with a strange enchantment. Charlotte's conscious state went blank. When she opened her eyes to her shock her lips were uniting with her sister's. She pushed her sister away from her yelling, "What the hell just happened?"

Lifting her face out of Charlotte's space, Denise responded, "I don't know. You were talking then you blacked out. Did you think I was coming on to you?"

"I would hope not." Charlotte sounding exasperated. "That would be gross. You are my sister."

Denise's expression changed from serious to her giggling. "Are you okay? You did just black out."

"I am fine. I just don't know what happened."

Charlotte began rubbing her temple trying to get a grip on her cluttered mind and shaken body. That's when she heard her sister's insinuations.

"Maybe you are curious." Denise continued to laugh.

Charlotte rose gingerly from the table, unsteady on her feet she was not fully aware of what had just happened. She opened the cabinet grabbing a glass and lowering it under the faucet while turning it on. Charlotte drank the cool water, then splashed some on her heated face. She turned back to her sister feeling uneasy about her latest question. Standing up straight not wanting to reveal how dizzy she really felt she proceeded to answer the question.

"No, sister dear. I am strictly dickly. I only desire men. Speaking of, I have an appointment with my boss this afternoon. So, you will be on your own with Beatrice. She won't bother you. She'll be in her room practicing her songs.

Still rubbing her temples, Charlotte noticed Denise's display of annoyance along with mumbling underneath her breath.

"You don't mind, do you? I will only be gone a few hours."

"Oh no. I was just saying how lovely Beatrice sings. It will be a joy to watch the girls for you today."

"It will be only Beatrice. She can take care of herself. Lucie has a date with Madeline soon. I hope Maddie hasn't forgotten. That's why I didn't bother to ask her about going with her father. I remembered Lucie promised to take her to the book fair that is being held in Haines City today. She enjoys her time with Lucie, but then books always win over fishing or anything else with Maddie."

Denise sashayed across the kitchen in front of Charlotte with a mischievous attitude asking, "I have noticed you spend plenty of time with your boss. Confess my darling sister. He is your lover, isn't he?"

Charlotte's face ignited with a redness from the sudden warmth the question produced. How could Denise have figured this out in the brief time visiting? Was it really that noticeable?

"No, he isn't my lover." She lied, but then immediately admitted, "Okay I confess. He is my lover. Not just my lover, my friend. I love him. Is it that obvious?"

"Absolutely. I knew the day of the funeral. The way he watches your every move. It's like you have him in a trance. I am surprised the wife hasn't caught on. Sister dear, you are so naughty." Denise brazenly replied.

Feeling her body shake even more with an added on twitch acknowledging the secret affair, Charlotte stared into Denise's eyes again. She started to feel dizzy once more. Releasing herself from her sister's glare she stumbled to sit back down at the dinette.

"Wow, what is wrong with me? I think I need to get a hot bath. Denise, you have to promise me that you will keep my secret to yourself."

Charlotte leaned her head on the table. Denise slowly turned around with a salacious grin on her face.

"Of course, I will. I love dirty little secrets." She winked. Her playfulness changed into a serious state turning back around to face Charlotte."

"Will you keep my secret too? It's not something I speak of. I just feel I can trust you. Somehow I feel you know the agony of being taken against your will."

"Of course, I will. I do understand." Charlotte hugged her sister with tears trickling down her face."

The moment was halted when Charlotte heard Madeline yell from outside announcing Lucie's arrival. The sliding glass door opened with her daughter and youngest sister entering. Madeline was excited about Lucie's arrival admitting she had forgotten about their book date. She happily skipped to her room to freshen up while declaring, "It is a wonderful day."

Lucie didn't acknowledge Denise's presence, she only noticed Charlotte wasn't herself.

"You alright? You kinda look pale Charlotte."

"I am fine. I just got a little dizzy before you got here."

"Are you sure? Do you need me to stay or take you to a doctor? Did Denise do something to you?"

Charlotte heard the huff of Denise's breath. If she didn't say something quick the two would engage in an argument that there was no time for.

"She's done nothing but try to help me. Loosen up Lucie."

Observing Lucie giving Denise the death stare, Charlotte knew the two would never get along. Lucie didn't like anything about their sister. She despised her strangeness and being gay didn't help matters. Lucie had a conspiracy theory about Denise concerning their mother's death. Lucie's paranoid delusion blamed Denise. Charlotte felt like it was the only way Lucie could deal with not going in the room to visit their mother before her passing. It was easier to blame the weirdo sister. Madeline entered the kitchen just in time to break the tension between the two sisters, which Charlotte was grateful for.

"Have fun Madeline. Enjoy your day with Lucie. I better go get dressed myself before I am late. Can't keep Mr. Lewis waiting forever."

She felt Lucie kiss her on the cheek before she left the house. Glaring at Denise with every step to the door, her younger sister finally stepped out to leave. As the glass door swiftly glided closed, Charlotte felt she should apologize once again for bad behavior.

"I am sorry. Lucie is protective of the children and me. I am sure when she gets reacquainted with you like I have, the both of you will act like sisters again. Her anger is not about you. It's herself she can't live with. Why don't I cancel my plans and we go do something together?"

She heard the snicker before Denise spoke, "So it's plans now not a meeting? Don't be ridiculous on both accounts. Lucie and I will never be friends nor sisters. Don't worry about me. Now go get ready to be with your man."

Continuing to tease Charlotte with a sexual growl.

The display made her giggle. She appreciated Denise's upbeat attitude even after her dark secret confession. Charlotte got up feeling much

better. Knowing she was going to be in Ridge's arms did that to her. Before leaving the kitchen to go get dressed, she reminded Denise,

"If you want some company, remember Beatrice is home."

Chapter Four

Hagen wiped the rain of bird poop the best he could from his clothing. His father tried to wipe while driving which turned out to be quite difficult. This bird attack was another of many strange occurrences that had lingered in their home since his grandmother's passing. The little things like the coffee table in the living room always finding its way in his path, no matter how he concentrated walking around it. To the noodles in his bowl hidden with maggots, with no explanation on how they got there. Then the day he was brushing his teeth spitting out the clear water that he had put in his mouth. Upon exiting, the water looked black as tar coming from his gurgling throat. He hadn't said anything to his family, but he always noticed a key element that was circulating around when the unsettling events occurred. Denise was always in the vicinity.

The truck veered off the highway on to a dirt road with the speed barely slowing down. The dust from the sandy road started swirling around them forming dust devils. The site startled Hagen yelling, "Look Dad."

His Dad looked into the rear view mirror while Hagen turned his body completely around by now to witness the bobbling dirt tornadoes. All he heard was his dad holler, "Holy shit. What the fuck is that?"

"A sign you need to slow down. Ya know? This is the road grandma's car accident happened on. They never really knew what made her hit the tree other than high speed. Which was not like her. Grandma never sped and hardly liked to drive."

Hagen knowing, he'd struct a nerve of an unwanted memory saw the foot of his father's lay off the gas pedal returning to a slower speed. With less speed, the dusty tornadoes abruptly evaporated.

"Dad, did you ever find out why Grandma was in such a hurry to get to your house?"

Looking away responding, "No I never did. Lilith was a woman of many mysteries. Who knows?"

They finally made it to the small cottage. It was surrounded by trees with vines along the branches. The kept up yard showed his Dad's presence on the property.

"Son. I think we need to go freshen up before we start to smell like something that'll scare off the fish. The stench of this shit is getting to my nostrils."

Jumping out of the truck with his camouflage duffle bag in hand, Hagen agreed. "Yes Sir. This smell of freshly deposited bird poop is not a very appealing fragrance."

Hagen walked in the tiny but neat home to trek straight to the spare room in the two bedroom home. He plopped his duffle on the standard size bed unzipping the bag to get some clean clothes out. With his clothes in his arms he exited the bedroom almost bumping into his father going into his own room.

"It will take me about five minutes to change," his Dad said closing the door.

"Same," Hagen responded entering the bathroom in the hall.

Five minutes later the two joined each other in the kitchen packing a few sandwiches and snacks for their day of fishing. Exiting the cottage Norman asked, "Do you wanna drive or walk."

"I think I would like to walk Dad. It's a nice day."

Getting their stuff loaded on their back while toting the other gear in hand, Father and son started their day. The silence between them was unusual but Hagen figured his father was tired.

"Are you okay Dad?"

"Yeah, sorry I am quiet. It's just when you brought up your grandma, it made me think about the night of the accident. I haven't thought of that night since the funeral. I try to keep it out of my mind. It still disturbs me."

Taking the one hand he had free, Hagen patted his Dad on the shoulder with understanding in his eyes. His Dad barely looked up nodding at him. The manly affection gave them both comfort. The light reflecting off the aqua blue sparkling lake made them stop in their tracks with his father announcing, "We are here."

They got out their fishing gear preparing the lines. Then threw their lines out into the water sitting back on the ground. There was nothing to do but wait for the fish to nibble the bait on the hooks.

The sounds of nature made the bank of the lake so relaxing. Hagen propped his arms behind his head with his legs stretched out to get more comfortable.

"You going to fish or take a nap boy?" His Father asked.

"It's so relaxing out here. It reminds me of sneaking in the bedroom with Beatrice and Maddie listening to the band of creatures outside."

"Band?" Norman said raising his eyebrow.

"Yeah, Beatrice would tell us there was a band made up of toads & owls that sang blue moon. It's funny the things we did to pass the evening hours."

He didn't even think before blurting the dialog. Hagen knew he had just reminded his Dad of another past he would rather forget.

"Dad, I am sorry. I didn't mean to bring that up."

Patting him on the shoulder, for the first time his Father admitted, "I was a bastard back then. I know."

Smiling to break the tension, he then asked.

"So, how's things going with Lezzy there?"

"Don't even get me started." Hagen groaned but continued.

"I can't stand her. I think she is weird. I overheard her talking to Mom about dancing on poles for men. It's disgusting. She's not even into guys. It is such a waste too. I mean Dad, have you looked at her? She is gorgeous until she opens that mouth. Aunt Denise is surely not a woman who knows her place." He snarled.

"Son listen to my advice. Don't go through life thinking women have a place. That was my mistake." His father counseled.

"Yeah, whatever." Hagen groaned again. "I just can't stand her. Since the day she arrived at the house strange things have occurred. I think she has something to do with it. She's pranking me or something."

Daddy began to laugh, "Careful Son, Lucie thinks Denise is a demonic entity summoned to bring us ill fortune."

"Do you believe in that stuff?" Hagen asked.

"You mean that magic stuff. I don't know. I have seen some weird stuff. But I am too busy trying to worry about real threats rather than ones I can't see or understand. Do I believe Denise had something to do with your grandmother's death like Lucie? No, I believe Lilith was speeding for some unknown reason. Unfortunately, she died. Blaming someone isn't going to bring her back. Sometimes people need to believe in something supernatural to explain their own faults. I wouldn't worry too much about it."

Feeling some confusion with his father's words, Hagen fired back. "So, you don't mind Denise being at the house?"

"Of course, I do. Not because of what she studies. It's because we really don't know her. Charlotte was never fond of her, now she is her friend. That concerns me. The last time your Mom trusted a stranger around my children, the price was paid. I know Beatrice and you can take care of yourself. It's Maddie I worry about. She needs to feel safe in her home. I don't understand why Charlotte doesn't make her leave. Did she not learn from Wendell? As your father, it's frustrating. I try not to be an asshole giving her the benefit of the doubt."

Hagen was about to speak when the line on his rod started bobbling. He got up trying to reel the fish in. His dad guided him for success of the capture. Reeling the huge fish in, father and son got excited about the catch. Norman lifted the hook from the fish's mouth with it flopping in his hands. Hearing his father's voice call out, "I wish Charlotte could see this." It made Hagen come to realize about his Dad.

His Dad's face was filled with pride when Hagen stared directly into his eyes asking, "You still love her after all that has happened?"

He watched his father's pride turn into a hidden hurt. Taking the fish hitting it in the head before putting it in the cooler on ice, he stood up facing Hagen.

"I will always love her. She is the mother of my children. The keeper of my soul. I ache for her. I know she will never be mine again. That is my fault. I have to carry that on my shoulders."

Feeling the sadness coming directly from his father's heart, all Hagen could say is "I'm sorry Dad."

"Don't be. I am okay. I still get the booty when I am in need." He laughed.

"Booty?"

"Yes booty. It's pussy, boy. I need to really tell you some things. Are you still a virgin?"

Hagen embarrassed by the question admitted, "I've had lips around it to make it spit, but nothing else."

"Okay, well you are almost there." His Dad laughed just as the lines on both rods started bobbling around.

The two reeled in more large size fish. Within the next hour, they had caught four more. They enjoyed their lunch on the bank while his Father told him stories of legends of the past. Hagen had dozed off again until feeling a slap on his leg. It was his father announcing it was time to leave.

"I think we have had a good day of fishing. Let's get to the house and cook these up for dinner, except the big boy. We will take it to the taxidermy to mount him on the wall." he boasted.

Walking back to the tiny dwelling, Hagen told his father he would cook the dinner while he got dressed. His father suddenly stopped turning asking, "Dressed for what?"

"I think you need to go out and get some booty. Quit being sad about Momma. Go have some fun." Hagen laughed, grinning like a Cheshire cat.

"What are you gonna do while I go get some booty." His father laughed.

"I will just watch a little television. I am tired."

"Are you sure?" He asked as they walked up to the house laying their gear outside. Opening the door carrying in the catch of the day to the sink to be cleaned, Hagen assured his father everything would be okay. Watching him grin, Dad headed to his room to shower."

Hagen walked over to the television where some videos sat on top of the television. The videos cardboard box covers displayed naked women bending over exposing themselves with a title across one of them called, "A hole lotta fun."

Hagen smirking stroking the box mumbled, "I am going to be just fine."

Chapter Five

Charlotte was excited to exit the dirt road leaving her home in the woods. She was going to her favorite place. The arms of her lover, Ridge Lewis. Though he had made no life commitments, time with him was her sanctuary. Knowing deep down, she was the woman he wanted his wife to be. None the less, she was deeply in love with him. He had been her savior in so many ways. Giving her a job when she desperately needed to rid herself of Norman, to protecting her from Wendell . when she was blind to him. Even now with loaning her a car until she decided to buy another one. The insurance company had cut her a check weeks ago for the car Momma had totaled. Sweet Ridge expressed to take her time finding a new one. He was in no hurry to get the car back. The car was quite cute and sportier than she was use too. The Mazda RX-7 was small but it grooved along the highway like a racecar. She enjoyed driving it. Pulling into the front of the office, she checked her look in the mirror reapplying glossy red lipstick. Giving her hair a quick shake, she lifted her boobs thinking to herself, "I am so ready for him." Feeling aroused, she got out of the car strutting in her silver stilettos into the office. The bell hanging from the door lightly rang as she stepped into the darkness of the entrance. The sensation of feeling arms reaching out, pulling her towards him. Ridge caressed her neck with his tongue whispering. "I have been waiting."

She wrapped her arms around his shoulders sliding her fingers through his sandy blonde hair. Ridge's eyes were filled with heated passion as he lifted Charlotte off her feet carrying her into his office. Placing her down, she faced him directly in the eyes. Brushing away her soft brown hair, he lifted the pink slinky easy to get out of dress over her head. Underneath, she wore a sexy slip that matched the dress along with complementing lacy under garments. He eased back for a moment staring.

She felt his warm moist breath in her ear.

"You like to tease me with these slips."

Turning to look him in the eyes murmuring, "I am still a lady, at least sometimes."

Charlotte began to kiss Ridge on his neck lifting the green polo shirt that complemented his Caribbean blue eyes over his head. Throwing his shirt to the floor while loosening his belt, she slid it out of the loops. Taking control of the belt, she popped it slapping his ass. He moaned with approval. Grabbing the belt from her, he stroked her arms clenching her wrists binding them with the belt he'd gained control of.

"It's not too tight." He asked coming out of the rest of his clothes, exposing his erection.

Charlotte knew at this moment she was completely under his control, but she trusted him. Smiling with erotic desire she commanded, "Tighter."

Coming closer to her, he tightened the belt around her wrist while maneuvering his fingers inside her slip. Releasing the bondage of her breast, he tore off the slip with her bra falling to the floor. The torn slip in his hands became a homemade blind fold tying it around her head. Charlotte could barely see him but felt him turning her around. Instructing her lean on the couch with her ass facing him. Her knees sank in the couch while her arms held on to the back on the couch. The sensation ignited her, feeling his fingers slipping inside her panties. Sliding the frilly panties off while fondling the lips of her mound, she started moaning. The pop of his hand on her ass gave her an erotic pleasure she never expected. Clutching her hands on the top of the couch, he slapped her three more times moistening her chamber with every whip. Ridge began licking the liquid appetizer she was providing. Charlotte moaned with sexual pleasure. She closed her blind folded eyes seeing images of being tied up with multiple men licking her. It made her arousal unbearable. Her screeching groans turned in screaming commands. "Fuck me Ridge, Fuck me now."

The hardness of his cock plunged into her with ravenous passion. The thrusts were hard and deep giving complete delight. His hands that had been holding on to her shoulders suddenly unleashed the belt binding her, turning her around to face him. Lifting his thighs in front of her lips she started jerking his cock with her unbound hands until he exploded in her face. Licking his passion juice, she arched her back with Ridge's finger's inserted inside her as she screamed out. The fingers gyrating the clitoris made her explode in wet ecstasy. Ridge rested his head in her lap huffing from the exertion. Charlotte rubbed her fingers through his blonde hair leaning her head against the couch.

"Oh, my Lawd, I needed that. "she confessed taking the blind off her eyes.

"I did too my wild cat." Ridge teased looking up with a grin.

"I wasn't too rough, was I?"

"No Baby, you were just right."

Charlotte began to giggle. She watched Ridge's smile begin to turn into a laugh. Looking at her, he asked "What are we laughing at?"

"I used to hate getting my ass beat before sex when I was married. Now I beg you to do it. The irony of it all makes me laugh." She continued to message his head with his hair between her fingers.

"We can stop if you want too. It was always your idea." Ridge softly replied.

"No. It just proves when gently done, it can be amazing. I was gonna ask for more. If you have the time?"

"I have the time."

Ridge winked laying her down on the couch lifting her legs to his shoulders inserting his once again stiff cock inside her. Charlotte was enjoying the slow rocking strokes she was receiving he when he suddenly stopped.

"Did you hear something?" he asked.

Leaning her head up to listen, she heard not a sound other than the cars driving by outside.

"It was probably the muffler of a car." Charlotte whispered.

Ridge turned his head looking around. Seeing nothing he engaged his mind back into pleasing Charlotte. Both engaging in erotic heaven, but unaware Ridge's wife was staring at them from behind the door of the entrance.

Chapter Six

The afternoon had nearly passed by the time Beatrice quit rehearsing. She had wanted to perfect the song *Angel of the morning* for an audition she was waiting on a call back for. The call if she was lucky would be from the local country band Southern Flare. She'd been dreaming of joining them for a long while now. Ever since she saw them play before her Uncle Bobby's band at the Pub and Grub, she had become obsessed to be part of the all-male group. The guys were in their twenties having a fresh flavor. She craved to be part of it but her youth and gender may detour their interest in her abilities as a singer. Lifting the stylus on the stereo, she carefully lifted the record off the turn table of the stereo. Placing the vinyl carefully back in its sleeve, she thought to herself, "One day someone will be playing a record of mine." After placing all her albums in their usual safe place, she straightened up the rest of her room. Tidying up everything including herself, the blonde hair, blue eyed songstress finally exited the bedroom. Roaming through the hallway, she glanced in every room along the hallway to see if anyone from her family was home. Momma had business with Mr. Lewis, Maddie had a date with Aunt Lucie, and Hagen was off with

Daddy. The only one left was her Aunt Denise. Beatrice wanted to get to know her, as much as she wanted to join the band. Much like the band, her chances for that may be limited but not for the same reasons. Her aunt seemed more fixated on Madeline more than anyone else. Which was unusual for Beatrice, other than Lucie others usually doted over her, not the quiet even nerdy at times bookworm Maddie. Hagen was a no brainer. Aunt Denise despised him, but Beatrice felt he deserved it. The constant remarks to her and nicknaming her Lezzy. She wouldn't expect anything but dislike for her brother from Denise.

Making her way through the living room into the kitchen she began to hum upon entry. Denise was standing at the stove stirring a pot of chili. Shockingly, the woman turned around welcoming, "Well hello humming bird."

Shocked at her friendliness, Beatrice cautiously answered, "Hello."

"I didn't think you would ever come out of your room."

Biting her lip Beatrice answered, "I'm sorry if my singing gets on your nerves. I just have to keep my voice strong."

Denise didn't even bother to ask. She dipped out some chili in a bowl placing it in front of her.

Then she commanded, "Don't nibble your lip. It will wrinkle it. Wrinkles my dear are sinful."

Beatrice watched as Denise poured herself a bowl placing it on the table. Then opening the cabinet for the crackers while grabbing two soda cans from the refrigerator, she joined her to eat the meal together. Speaking the words Beatrice had longed to hear, her aunt announced her intentions.

"Well it looks like it's just you and me for a while. Everyone is off doing their own things. My humming bird niece and I should get to know each other."

"I'd like that." Beatrice expressed.

"Okay then. You go first. Tell your Auntie about yourself. I know you sing but what are your desires?"

Beatrice had wanted for weeks to have a one on one conversation. Now that is was happening, it felt like her tongue was tied. All she could

evolve from her throat was the one word question, "Desires?"

"Yes. Desires. Everyone has them."

A feeling of sudden nervousness took over her calm. "I want to marry Scott one day." She stuttered.

"Oh, good grief humming bird. Have more ambition than that. A man will get in the way of anything you want to do or accomplish. You should rid yourself of him quick as you can. He's kinda of a dweeb anyways."

The table became silent for a few minutes before Beatrice responded to her aunt. Looking up at her with the bluest of still innocent eyes she answered, "But I love him."

Denise placed her hand on top of Beatrice's. She chanted some words that Beatrice didn't understand before speaking again to her.

Caressing her cheeks, Denise's iniquitous but serious remarks seized Beatrice's attention.

"I know you think you do. Don't settle on the first one. Considering your eyes, I know he is not even the first one yet. You have been

thinking of it. I am just trying to advise you. Why settle on the small woods when there is a huge forest out there with many possibilities of seeds to be planted?"

Still stuttering Beatrice repeated, "But I love him. You act as though you know things."

It was then when she noticed the book sitting in front of Denise. The book was a dirty brown. Its texture was rough as though it had been passed on for decades.

"Do you know these things from reading this book? Does the book tell you our future?" Beatrice asked now with a curious strength in her voice having no sounds of stuttering.

Her aunt's black curls flopped in front of her face hunkering over in laughter.

"No humming bird, this is my book of spells. Some can tell futures through the cards. I can by nature. I depend on the Goddess for guidance. The `breezes of the wind guides me to my knowledge. I dance at night to honor the Goddess for my wisdom. The ability to read is a gift. The cards can be taught."

"Auntie can you teach me? The cards? How to pray to the wind?"

"If that's what you desire. Yes, youngling I can teach you." Pointing her painted red nails up she also advising Beatrice of something she knew was also true.

"I shouldn't ask but whatever I teach you, it has to stay between us. Your Momma may not approve. So, if you can keep yer mouth quiet, I would love to be your advisor."

Beatrice's eyes widened with enthusiasm. She felt her bottom lift with excitement that guided her in the arms of Denise.

The laughter from her aunt's approval deafened the room. Feeling Denise pull away from her, she became embarrassed of her eagerness that reflected her age. Auntie spoke invading her every thought. Beatrice wanted to learn this trait.

"Humming Bird, your readiness to learn excites me. You don't mind me calling you humming bird, do you?"

"No, I think it is sweet. When can you start teaching me?"
"Is now too soon?" Denise asked with her own enthusiasm.

"No." Beatrice eagerly shouted.

"Then let's begin."

Chapter Seven

There were dozens of books shelved everywhere at the downtown community center. Lucie captured the thrill of it in Maddie's eyes stroking each book walking by the displays. Admiring each like she had just uncovered lost treasure.

Lucie kept quiet as Madeline would pick up a book skimming through it. After a few seconds of admiration, she would walk on to the next all the whilst shooting grins toward her aunt.

Walking behind her niece, she rubbed her delicate shoulders.

"You know Maddie, you can pick a few to buy. It's my treat to you."

"Really?" The young girl expressed gratitude with a fist pump.

"Yes, really. Now what do you want to pick?"

"Everything." Madeline giggle.

"Well I can't afford everything, but how about three? Will that cure your appetite for a bit." Lucie smiled.

"Yes, Aunt Lucie, thank you so much." Madeline said with excitement.

Lucie and Madeline was looking through the selections of books when they heard a voice echo through the crowd yelling, "Lucie."

Looking up, Lucie kept staring but didn't see anyone she was acquainted with. Hearing the voice once more, she scanned the room searching for the face responsible for voice blaring her name. Approaching her was a familiar face with a different look. Lucie stared at the woman realizing it was Sharon. Her long brown locks transformed to bleached blonde with the shortest of pixie cuts. Being surprised by her latest style, her only response, "Wow. Look at you."

"Do you like it?" Sharon asked while twirling around in a denim dress wearing white cowgirl boots that complimented the western accessories she was wearing.

"I love it." Having to ask, Lucie propping her hands on her hips, "Now you better have a damn good reason on why you didn't come to my shop."

"I wanted to surprise you." She giggled.

"Well I am surprised. How does Bobby like your new look?"

Lucie noticed Sharon's facial expression trailed off from happy to discontent. Her sister tried to fake it by displaying a smile fake as the joker's lipstick grin. It made her wonder about Sharon's sudden appearance change.

"He hasn't seen it yet. It just happened a few hours ago. I love it. I hope he will too."

"I'm sure he will, Hun." Expressed Lucie feeling her sister needed some encouragement.

Sharon took a few minutes to greet Madeline. Lucie proudly watched Madeline showed off the books she had selected to purchase. Sharon flipped through them stopping at one announcing, "Well that's interesting."

Before Lucie could glance at the selections, Sharon interrupted with several questions.

"So, where's Dan? Did he go fishing with Norman and Hagen? That's where Bobby is now. They have been having gatherings quite frequent don't ya think?"

Lucie was confused by all the questioning. Dan had been gone no more than usual lately. Nothing that concerned her. Sharon was acting like a stressed suspicious woman.

"Dan has always gone fishing, Sis. Is there any reason why I should think different?"

"I guess I am having newlywed anxiety. We used to do everything together. Now we are married, we have settled down. I miss the spontaneous adventures. I guess I made the change to spice up things."

"It will be okay. No one can be newlyweds forever. But it's good to change every now and then, it keeps them guessing." Lucie conveyed with a wink.

Turning to Madeline, Lucie asked if she was ready to pay for the books. With her nieces' grin as an answer words didn't need to be spoken. They all walked to the long line of other book lovers waiting to purchase their selections.

"Are you taking Maddie home once you are finished here?"

"No, I am taking her to dinner and some ice cream for desert. Noah is going off with your Sammy, while Dan is off fishing too. It's just me spending time with Maddie. You can join us if you want?"

"Well, I was thinking about going out to Charlotte's later and hoped maybe we could just ride together or something." Sharon said with a little disappointment in her voice.

"Well, Charlotte isn't even home right now. Just Beatrice and the evil one, Denise. I don't care to be around her at all. So even if I went, I wouldn't be staying long."

"Oh, that's right. Denise is still here. I've been thinking maybe we should be like Charlotte and try to get to know her."

Lucie gritted her teeth trying not to curse around young Madeline. She couldn't control her finger that started pointing in Sharon's direction indicating her loath of their sister with harsh words.

"Even if hell were to freeze over I would never hang with that wicked witch."

"Well does it really matter because from my point of view Charlotte and I aren't that close either. I have been thinking maybe I shouldn't be so harsh on Denise. She probably tolerates me more than Charlotte ever could. I think I will drive out there. I need to relay a message to Beatrice that a band she is auditioning for asked me to give her. I've tried calling but no one answers. I have nothing to do anyways."

Lucie raised her eyebrow displaying her disapproval.

"I asked you to join us."

"I know. I am just not really up to eating right now, or ice cream."

Sharon kissed Lucie on the cheek then bent down to kiss Madeline on hers. She said her good byes in a haste leaving as fast as she had arrived.

Madeline gazing at Sharon disappearing in the crowd looked up at Lucie. "What's wrong with her? She was being kinda strange."

"You noticed that too, Maddie?"

Madeline appeared annoyed for a second but nonchalantly addressed her observance.

"I may be just a kid but, I know when people seem off. It's in their eyes. In her eyes, I see discontent, worry, even jealousy. Ya know like in Aunt Denise's eyes the fire tells me her true soul is wicked."

Lucie's legs felt stiff hearing her niece confess her words. Madeline could see things the way she could. The expression on her face revealed to her niece, she could see it too. Her excitement surfaced again, "Auntie you can see it too?"

"I can Maddie. I have never mentioned it to anyone but Father Carson. Now let's pay for these books and get out of here. We have plenty to discuss.

****

Lucie stopped to use the payphone outside the community center. Madeline asked if she could go on to the car parked just a few rows where Lucie was using the phone. Being in clear view, she agreed watching her niece skip all the way until she was secured in the car. Lucie opened her purse in search of a dime. Scuffling at the bottom, she snagged the coin. Her hands were shaking dropping the coin in the slot quickly dialing the numbers. The male voice that answered the phone was calm unlike hers. The erratic tone in hers was alarming. The man suggested she come and share dinner with him. The phone went silent a few seconds before accepting the invite. Agreeing to come, Lucie slammed the phone down.

Rushing to her car opening the door, she eased herself inside. Noticing Maddie already had her nose in one of the books, Lucie saw the alarming cover. The book titled, "Understanding the occult." In impulse, she grabbed the book slamming it shut.

"Maddie, why would you buy this book?" Lucie scolded.

"I'm sorry Auntie. I just thought if I understood, maybe I could fight it. I know it has something to do with the fire in Denise's eyes. I am trying to find the answers."

Lucie took the book tucking it underneath her seat. Taking a deep breath, she cranked the ignition starting the engine. Putting the car in reverse to back out, whisking the steering in circular motion. Changing the gear to drive, they sped out of the community center.

"I didn't mean to upset you." She heard her niece softly say. Please don't take me home.

Feeling ashamed for her harshness, Lucie apologized. It wasn't Madeline's fault for not knowing what the book she bought could bring. The book was as evil as her sister. She was thankful she had changed their dinner plans pulling into parking lot at the Catholic

Cathedral. Her niece was surprised and a little confused to why they were there.

"Aunt Lucie, I thought you said we were going out to eat? You are still mad at me? Aren't you?"

Lucie placed her hand on Madeline's conveying, "No child, I am not angry. We are here to get your answers. It will protect you."

Holding up the book Maddie had purchased, putting it under her arm. She swiftly opened the door explaining, "Sweetie, this book will only make things worse. We need to get rid of it. C'mon, there's someone in here I want you to meet."

The two entered the quiet sanctuary holding hands. Lucie knew the place frightened her niece even though it was a house of God. Her trembling hands told her story of fear. The echo of Father Carson's voice entered the center aisle where they stood in front of the alter. The brown wooden cross hung over them made the jerking in the palm of Madeline's hand settle.

"Hello Lucie. It's a pleasure to share the evening with you tonight. Who is this beautiful girl you have brought with you?" Father Carson asked with a gentle timbre.

"This is my niece Madeline. My sister's Charlotte's youngest child." Lucie introduced.

"She is beautiful like her mother. I have dinner on the table. Would you like to join me in my quarters?"

Before Lucie could respond to the invitation, Madeline curiously asked, "We are eating here?"

The priest butted in this time before she could respond, "Yes child, I have prepared an exquisite dinner for your aunt and you. The entrée is pizza."

"Pizza is exquisite!" smiled Madeline.

"Yes, when it's homemade." He winked gently laughing. "Now, please come join me."

Lucie walked with the priest to his quarters. Along the way, they passed lit candles honoring all the saints. When they passed

Michael, Madeline suddenly stopped. She turned from them bowing to the Angel. Turning back to them announcing, "He is much more beautiful than this."

The announcement startled Father Carson and her. The priest remained silent while opening the door to his tiny living space. In the candle lit room was a small round table with three chairs placed around it. Though small it was set like a fancy restaurant waiting on royalty. Everything on it shined. In the center of the table he had placed a glass vase with three red roses. The view of the setting was beautiful.

Lucie sat when Father Carlson scooted the chair out for her as he did with Madeline. Using a pie knife he lifted the already cut pizza placing a piece of the homemade cuisine on their plates. It was made up of marinara sauce, pepperoni, green peppers, and onions all covered in gooey cheese. The aroma from the Italian pie made the atmosphere seem like they were in Rome. The priest then placed bowls of salads in front of them. He seated himself placing his hands out to theirs announcing, "Now we pray."

After the prayer, Lucie lifted her head, looking at the priest saying, "Amen" with Madeline following with her own innocent amen passing through her lips. They began to eat the feast he had made for them. Lucie was waiting for Father Carson to start the conversation. Being the young one, her niece not waiting, began to speak.

"This is delicious. It's exquisite like you said. Thank you for making us such a wonderful meal. Do you have ice cream too?"

Her youthful innocence made Lucie and him laugh. The innocence made the room calm of all the worries that revolved around. Until the meal was finished, they enjoyed each other's company with simple small talk. When Madeline finished her ice cream, Father Carson cleared his throat to begin to speak. Lucie sat listening to him engage a more serious conversation.

"Your aunt has told me some interesting things about you. I hope you trust me enough to share what you see with me as you did with her."

Madeline's smile beamed at Father Carson. Lucie knew why her smile was bright, she saw the goodness in him. She remained quiet not to interrupt the two in conversation.

"I do trust you." Madeline answered.

"Good. Then child tell me about all that you see."

"I've seen things since I can remember. The fire just recently. I saw it in the bad man's eyes. I see that same fire in my Aunt's eyes. I bought a book, so I could learn why I see fire in her eyes, but Lucie took it from me. That's why we are here. But what she doesn't know is whether I read that book or not the answers someday will be revealed to me. I am not afraid for he is by my side."

Lucie glanced up at Father Carson. His eyes looked directly at her. They were both equally curious to Madeline's words.

"Aye. You are correct. Our Father in Heaven is always with us. The power is yours when you are not afraid. Remember that."

"That's what he says." Madeline calmly blurted back.

"He? Is he someone other than our Father?" The priest asked with curiosity.

"Yes. The angel. Sir Michael. But he doesn't want me to call him that, just Michael." She gushed.

Lucie's silence was so discreet. One would have never known of her presence, had not she'd been sitting at the table. She continued to listen and stare at the priest every time Madeline spoke.

"How long has Michael visited with you?" Father Carson asked.

"For long as I can remember. He is so beautiful and kind. He saved me from the mean man. He knows of Denise. Michael says I am protected. To call out to him or just think of him, and he will come to my aide. My thoughts of him tonight have brought him here. If you look up, the light is not from the candle. It beams from his glorious presence."

Lucie and Father Carson glanced up becoming startled seeing the brightness of the ceiling. The shadow reflected a man's body with his wings fully displayed. The priest collapsed to his knees with Lucie following. Praying to the angel, Lucie couldn't help but to stare up at the ceiling.

"Isn't he beautiful Aunt Lucie." Madeline praised.

The light lifted with the shadow disappearing. The questions vanished from Lucie's thoughts still in shock of what she had just witnessed.

Father Carson grazed Madeline's forehead with his hand praying. Lucie knew something had revealed itself to him by the way his fingers started trembling. Standing back on their feet, he asked if they wanted to go outside on the terrace. They all left the table walking into the moonlit rose garden. Madeline's face filled with elation seeing the water fountain flowing into the sparking water underneath it. She entertained herself gliding her fingers across it while the priest spoke to Lucie.

"Father, how do you explain what just happened? What does it mean?"

"It means the prophecy is true. It has begun."

"What has begun? What prophecy? Lucie demanded to know.

"The prophecy that God will have pure souls born to the arch angels to help them fight the final battle. No one talks of it. I don't know if the Vatican really believes it."

"Why wouldn't the Vatican believe, if it is the word of God?"

"Because it was never written in the word of God. Nothing of it. There have been ones under demonic possession to speak of the coming of pure souls. They have all vowed to kill them."

Lucie could feel the twitch taking over her body like a frigid wind had just hit her. The scene of her niece was magnificent. Every step she took around the fountain grazing the water was a shining light following her.

"Father Carson, you think Madeline is a pure soul?"

"I think she is." He confined.

"Then she is protected?"

"She is a protected target. They will keep coming for her. Not just the coven, but demonic entities as well. The coven cursed the family before Madeline was conceived. They knew as Michael did the very day her pureness was born to the earth. You must keep a watch on the girl. It would explain the fire in your sister's eyes. The witches have gotten to her. As long Madeline is aware of it, they can't hurt her."

"But what about Charlotte and this book?" Lucie asked holding up the book with fear in her voice.

"That's why I ask you to watch over her. Continue to pray for your sister. The angel will protect Madeline. The girl loves her mother. The pureness running through her veins, she would offer herself to save her mother. That's why she is being guarded by the highest of admirals in God's army. As for that book, give it to me. I will destroy it."

Lucie could feel the grip of Father Carson's arm come around her shoulder to embrace her while confiscating the book. Leaning towards her ear, he whispered.

"Even if the coven can't consciously get Charlotte to join, they can hypnotize her into things she wouldn't normally do. Which puts Madeline at risk. Her not believing in the darkness makes her an unknowing participate in their evil."

"Are you sure Father? Madeline is one of these pure souls?" Lucie gasped.

They paused in silence watching Madeline playing with a rare butterfly she had caught in the garden. The wings were blue trimmed in black. The blue morpho was not a species to North America. Looking at the unique winged creature in her hands was the confirmation Lucie needed.

As she let the beautiful butterfly go, the priest turned to Lucie answering, "Yes I do."

Lucie's mouth fell open learning the revelation. The priest revealed more whispering in her ear.

"Not only will the witches come after her. Like I said, the demons will too. They all seek to destroy her. If the witches should fail, the demons will never give up. They will slither through any crack to get to her. Do you understand?"

Trembling in fear, Lucie's only responded, "Yes, Father."

Chapter Eight

The dirt road to Charlotte's house was foggy as Sharon drove into the woods. The light breeze rustled the branches of the oak trees that hummed a mystical tune. Her headlights bounced off the ground to the view of the woods with every bump she hit. Slowly releasing her foot from the gas pedal, she idled down the sandy road. In the glare of the headlights she saw the image of a woman dressed in a Victorian black dress. The woman of ebony decent was enchanting as she appeared to float on her feet. When she turned to face Sharon, her eyes were ignited like fire. With the shock of the vision that passed before her eyes, Sharon slammed on the breaks in a sudden panic.

Shaking her head, then gripping the steering wheel, she murmured, "Get a grip. You are letting your mind go." Then with an erratic laugh she raved, "I am sure Momma is loving this. Me losing my shit. Even in her death, I can't rid myself of her."

She slowly eased her car into Charlotte's driveway. Like Lucie had said, her sister was nowhere on the property. The house was dark displaying no indication that anyone was home. Sharon got out of her car to knock on the door. When no one answered, discovering the door was unlocked. She walked in calling for Beatrice. There was no one in the house as she scanned every room in search of her niece. She sat on the couch staring at Charlotte's beautiful home. It seemed like she had all the fortune in life. No matter how bad things got for precious Charlotte, things always worked out for her. Even in the final days of Momma's life, their Momma would react more to Charlotte's voice than any other. Seeing the response to her sister made her develop a jealousy for Charlotte she never had experienced. She was the one who had taken care of Momma all these years. The betrayal of Momma with her husband. Despite it, she still loved her unlovable mother. In the end, nothing mattered to good ole Momma but her precious Charlotte. Nothing stung her heart more than this. It was the last thing to finally break her. The venom had poisoned her peaceful soul. It was starting to affect her new once happy marriage. Since Lilith's passing the arguments came out of nowhere with Bobby. He left more than he stayed with her. Glancing at her sparkling diamond that surrounded her left finger beside the gold band, the jealousy towards her sister was revolving more into anger. Sitting in the dark in her sister's lovely living room, she decided it was best to leave. As

she closed the unlocked door, walking out to her car she could see a fire flickering in the back of the woods of Charlotte's secluded home. Her thoughts of wonder made her sneak into the woods to see what was going on. She paced slowly so her footsteps couldn't be heard from her stepping on the crunchy leaves and limbs that had fallen. This year the dropping acorns were more scattered across the ground. It appeared the squirrels had gotten lazy doing their jobs of gathering. Finally making her way to the fire what she saw stunned her. She watched in silence as Denise and Beatrice stood in front of the fire chanting something about a Goddess. It frightened her, but it strangely intrigued her as well. Overcoming her fear, she broke through the tangle of vines that concealed her presence, falling to her knees from the spectacle she was witnessing. The chants ceased as she looked up demanding, "What is this?"

Denise approached her with glazed eyes speaking in a way that made her sound snooty and eccentric.

"Well hello Sister dear, have you been creeping around, or are you wanting to join in?"

Still on the ground, scooting away from her strange sister, Sharon sat up dusting the debris from her knees.

"I am not creeping," she explained standing to her feet. "I was here to deliver a message to Beatrice. Seeing no one was home, I was about to leave when I saw the flames of the fire."

Crossing one arm over the other, while resting her chin on her hand, Denise stared at Sharon like she could see into her soul. The words she spoke made her feel that the sister read into her personal thoughts.

"You have come to join us. Curiosity is what brings you here despite your fear. Even though frightened, you are feeling an exhilaration you have never experienced. What is it sister dear? The fire, the praise to the Goddess, or well let's not get into the that." Denise wickedly winked distributing a cackling laugh.

"No, you are wrong on all three." Sharon countered back.

"I only mentioned two."

Beatrice began to speak with excitement but also vigilant for Sharon to keep her silence of what she had just witnessed.

"Aunt Sharon, what you have seen here is us praying for my good will. I have been nervous about some things. These chants are only to help bring me peace along with prosperity. But you must not tell Momma. She would not understand."

Sharon still unsure of what was happening shifted her attention to her niece. She handed the piece of paper that was sent from the band for her. Beatrice read the paper that made her pupils pulsate with anticipation. Grabbing her, hugging her tightly, Beatrice whispered.
"Auntie it's already working. The chant is bringing my dream closer to me."

Sharon observed her niece then bow to Denise, before tuning to walk towards home.

"What did the note say?" Sharon asked.

"My audition is at noon tomorrow. I prayed to the Goddess for it to happen. Then you show up with this. Maybe Denise can bring you good fortune too."

"Why are you leaving?" Sharon continued with questions.

"Because the note says to call them to discuss what song I want to sing. Good night Auntie's. I have much to do."

Beatrice ran through the crispy leaves not caring what sounds she made.

Sharon hollered out, "Beatrice be careful. I saw something out there tonight."

Her niece only threw her hand up indicating she had no fear of anything in the woods. Sharon turned to Denise frightened but still intrigued. Knowing her sister already sensed her concern, she asked the question going closer to the fire.

"What is Beatrice talking about? What are you teaching her?"

Denise was wearing a black dress that firmly buttoned up around the top of her exposed bosoms. Wearing a matching black cloak, she lifted the hood releasing her wild long black locks. She walked in circles around her. Denise's piercing blue eyes made Sharon's skin tingle. She spoke in a language she didn't understand. Stroking her face, beginning to make her body feel some strange arousal that prompted Sharon to back away.

"Don't fight it Sister. Come to me. Release all your fears, anger, and jealousy. You will live in peace."

"I don't even know what you are talking about?" Sharon shouted.

"I will teach you. I will guide you as she guided me." Denise confessed.

"Is that what you are doing to Beatrice?"

"Beatrice will do great things. She is young though. Yes, I do intend to teach her. That is if you don't tell Charlotte. But I don't think it's an issue, your energy reveals a discontent of our sister."

"I don't know what you are talking about."

Denise invaded her space glaring into her eyes. She felt hands come around her body guiding her closer to her sister. The flare from her eye's left blindness with only darkness. Feeling soft lips on the skin of her neck, her heart began to race. Unable to stop it, she relinquished trying to resist. Hands slid down her waist grabbing the end of her dress removing the denim over her head. Fingers released her breasts from the bondage of her bra. Never had she experienced this erotic feeling of euphoria. She felt the fingers trail around to her nipples. A tongue slipping across each licking her aroused erect tips. The darkness in her sight turned into visions of the ebony woman seducing her. Sharon's body had never felt so passionate but most of all peaceful. Enjoying every stroke of the woman's finger inside her she released the breath she was holding still unable to move. A red flash came before her eyes returning to herself. When her vision came clear to her again, Denise was standing in front of her staring. They were both fully clothed which confused Sharon.

"What just happened." Sharon softly asked.

"The mystical magic of the night just invaded your soul. You have been given an enlightenment to a different world. Do you still want to resist?"

Sharon's heart still pounding from the experience. She yearned for more. Without any thought or hesitation, she answered, "I want this peace. Share it with me."

Together hand in hand, the sisters stood in front of the fire. The flames flickered shooting sparkling ash. A sign that the coven was growing stronger.

Chapter Nine

Bobby sat alone on the bank of the lake waiting for Dan to show. He sipped his beer hoping the alcohol would ease his anxiety. It had been weeks since Sharon had lost her Mom. Some days if felt like his wife had lost her mind with the shock of the loss. His happy marriage had turned into dreaded chaos. There was a time when he thought Lilith was to blame for all the commotion. Now it appeared only Sharon brought the drama into their home. Her constant blabbering about how in the final days her Momma had mostly responded to Charlotte. If he had to hear the jealous rant one more time, he feared his temper would finally explode. Never wanting to go down the path of his brother, rather than hit a woman. He would just leave. The leaving brought on even more of a ruckus. Now he was being accused of cheating. He had never been so faithful to a woman in his entire life as he had been to Sharon. She had no merit in her accusations. Yet the arguing never ceased. It was getting ridiculous. Along with his cock constantly aching from not being attended too. He had never masturbated so much. The wind rustled taking his attention off his thoughts. The ripples on the lake formed from the breeze blowing. It gave him a moment of peace to watch. Bobby stared listening to the sounds of the chirping crickets nearby. Hearing footsteps shuffling in the leaves from the distance, he glanced up to see his tall, long, and lanky brother-in-law hike towards him. Reaching his destination beside him, Dan placed his gear down while asking, "I thought we were going fishing with Norman and Hagen?"

Bobby opened the cooler filled with beer, throwing a cool one at Dan.

"We were but Norman said something about bringing Maddie along and needed to spend some alone time with his kids. I figured it would be best if we went alone. Anyways, if he brings his little girl with him, she doesn't need to be around a bunch of foul mouth men."

Dan hunched down on his knees to sit next to Bobby responding, "Oh, I see what ya mean. We are foul mouth. Speaking of, how long you been out here fucker?" he snickered.

Dan popped open his can of brew getting settled in the dirt propping his back alongside the trunk of a tree that had fallen close to the bank. Bobby realized his buddy didn't even set up his gear to fish.

"You're not fishing today?"

"I am just enjoying the quiet. Things have been busy at home. I need to relax more than fish." Dan responded.

"Things have been chaotic at your house too?" Bobby asked.

"Yeah a little more than usual. Ya know Lucie is so feisty. It's always a little crazy. But if I have to hear the legend of the curse one more time, I think I am gonna lose my shit. I know it by heart now. Her Momma's death has made it evolve into all kinds of conspiracies. Lucie has always been fixated about the story, but now it is interrupting things."

"Interrupting things?" Bobby curiously responded. "Like what?"

"Ya know. Like things. Like my dick ain't getting wet as much. She is too busy gabbing about the curse. Before bedtime, she has to pray it off. Doesn't make for a night of romance. Ya know what I mean?" Dan chuckled.

Bobby leaned his head down. He knew exactly what he meant adjusting his swollen scrotum.

"Yeah there hasn't been much action at my home either. At least you aren't getting accused of cheating when you feel like your balls are gonna explode. I mean the rosy palm helps, but it still doesn't make you release like a warm piece of pie."

"Or like the suction of cherry gloss lips." Dan commented. The two men high fived their hands in the air with dirty grins stretched from side to side.

After a few amusing exchanges back and forth to each other, it suddenly became quiet.

Dan set his gear up casting his line into the lake. Propping his rod into the sand securing it with the tree trunk, he had previously rested on. Bobby decided to go search for wood to build a fire. Since it was obvious neither of the men were in a hurry to return home.

The search for wood took Bobby deeper in the secluded wooded area. The squeaking calls of the squirrels entertained him as he watched the rodents run up and down the trees. A fawn appeared in its radiant grace until it became spooked by the chirps of the birds that alerted the animal of his presence. Thinking to himself, "You are safe girl. I don't have my gun and I don't shoot females."

As he got deeper in the woods, Bobby came upon a pile of limbs stacked perfectly. They appeared to be left for him, abandoned by someone who probably got spooked. Feeling lucky to find limbs, he bent down to pick up the bundle of good fortune. Noticeably, the sounds of the woods went strangely quiet. Feeling a presence, he stood back up with a vision of beauty appearing before him. A woman of color became visible. Her shimmering skin glowed of honey. At first, he thought she was a ghostly hologram until she touched his arm with her delicate hand. Admiring her outfit, she was dressed in a camouflage jumpsuit with long silky black hair hanging out of the *Indiana Jones* style wool fedora. Her gold eyes were hypnotizing. Her hour glass figure fit the tight jumpsuit perfectly. Her plump breast perked out of the zipped down outfit. She smiled at him with her terracotta sweet lips. He instantly wondered what her lips tasted like before she even spoke a word.

"Are you taking my wood?" She softly asked.

"Oh sorry, Ma'am. I didn't realize it was yours or that anybody else was out here. It is kinda secluded."

"I like secluded."

Bobby stared at her in confusion to why she was out in the middle of the woods. Not only that, she was bare footed.

"Are you lost?"

The woman began to laugh further drawing him into the mystery with her hypnotizing eyes that had put his mind into almost a fog.

"I told you I like seclusion. So, no I am not lost. You took my wood, now I have to take your soul."

"What?"

Her teeth sparkled white as she started to howl in laughter.

"I am kidding but I would like my wood back. I see you don't have much humor."

"I have plenty of humor Ma'am. I am just not use to finding a beautiful woman roaming around barefoot in the woods. What brings you out here?"

She leaned into his shoulder whispering, "You." The scent her body revealed itself all the way to his loins. She walked away from him then tuned back towards him.

"Are you taking me to your camp or are you gonna leave a damsel alone in the woods."

"No. I mean yes Ma'am. You are welcome to follow me. I have a friend with me. If you don't mind more company."

"The more the merrier." She winked leading him back to the lake where Dan was waiting.

Bobby felt like he must be in a dream until they made it back to the lake. The mysterious woman knew exactly where they had been fishing. He was starting to get a bad feeling about it. Seeing Dan's shocked expression confirmed he was wide awake. Dan's eyes grew wider as they got closer.

"Look what I found in the woods." Bobby announced when approaching him.

"Is she lost?" Dan asking the same question as he had.

"No, I am not lost." The woman answered. "Is that what men think? That little ole women can't take care of themselves in the scary woods."

"No, Ma'am. It's just not every day like I said that I just find one in the woods alone." Bobby retorted again.

"Please, is your name Bobby? Don't refer to me as Ma'am. It sounds so old. Dead almost. I am young. Vibrant." Her soft erotic voice echoed intoxicating his ears.

"How do you know my name?"

She ignored the question asking, "Are you gonna build a fire or not."

Bobby shrugged his shoulders confused. Dan began to build the fire not looking at the unwelcomed woman. Within just a few moments the sunset, and the fire was lit.

"If you don't want to me to call you Ma'am. Then what do you prefer us to call you."

The woman gave a malicious grin that told his soul he should run as fast as he could out the woods. The glow of her enchanting body screamed at him to stay. Dan didn't give any indication of going anywhere either.

"My name is Amorita, but Amora will do."

The woman stood by the fire. The slight breeze of wind blew her hair along with the rhythm of the blazing flames. She unzipped her jumpsuit coming out completely nude. Feeling the nervous impulse to run again, Bobby asked "What are you doing? How do you know my name?"

"I know everything. I am the Goddess of the night."

Dan began to laugh so hard he held onto his sides.

"Okay what kind of wacky tobacky have you been smoking lady? We can help you if you are lost. But put on your clothes."

Bobby could see the anger flare in the beautiful one's eyes. She screamed in a language neither man understood. The impulse again emerged to run. He could see himself running in his mind, yet his body stayed still. Fear invaded his spirit realizing he was unable to move. Only able to stand up straight, he felt stiff as a corpse. Bobby tried to yell to Dan, but his vocal cords had been stripped silent. In horror, he watched the woman brake out in dance chanting, "Accipe sacrificium nocte ad patrem meum."

By the third repeated chant Bobby saw Dan's face turn a pale white. He tried to run but the woman's hair turned to strands of snakes. The serpents slithered off her body tripping Dan in his attempted escape. Falling to the ground, the snakes spread his arms and legs out rapping their bodies tight around him, so he could not move. Bobby watched horrified as the sand around Dan swirled until it formed a pentagram encircling his body. The woman crawled her naked body over him pulling his pants to his knees. A hurling wail came from her throat stroking his dick until it was hard.

Throwing her hips over his thighs, she pounded his cock with the thrusts of her pussy. Dan tried to scream but the serpent crawled in his month quieting his cries. The black birds squawked above until she climaxed. In horror, Bobby stared unable to move or speak hearing the woman chant again, "Accipe sacrificium nocte ad patrem meum."

A fire lit up from the ground starting to burn Dan's hands and feet. The sand tunneled between his legs opening a portal where a horned terrifying creature emerged yanking off Dan's head gulping it down his throat.

Bobby had no choice but to watch. The woman, he now knew as Amora from the wind whispering her name. She was a Goddess. One from hell. The truth surfaced, she was in the woods waiting for him. Not just him, but his soul. He knew at that moment all the urban legends of the curse were true. Amora glided over to him removing his pants. The suction of her lips covered his dick in blood. He saw the marking of evil. The fire lit up around Bobby. He was powerless to run watching the pentagram form with fire circling around him. The chants of Accipe sacrificium nocte ad patrem meum," exhaled from Amora's lungs. The words released to his ears hearing the chant translate, "receive the sacrifice of the night to my Father."

 Seeing the tunnel coming, he prayed, "God help me."

Chapter Ten

From the window, Hagen watched the headlights of his Father's truck leave the cottage in the woods. Finally, alone he took the VHS tape out of its case sliding it in the recorder. It wasn't long before the moans of the woman echoed from the television's speakers. The erotic tape had his mind spinning but was interrupted by a thundering knock at the door. From the couch, he tried to see if anyone was standing in view of the window. Not seeing anyone, he ignored it. The knock became louder and persistent, Hagen had no choice but to answer the nuisance. Suspecting it was his cousins who had mentioned they might drop by, all he could think of is what an awkward time to have to answer the door. Adjusting himself making sure he wasn't standing in straight embarrassing attention, he hesitantly cracked the door peeking through. Feeling the added tightness of his jeans, the heart equally tightened when a woman dressed in camouflage stood in the door way.

"Can you help me?"

Standing, feeling startled he responded, "If I can, Ma'am."

The beautiful woman had a captivating smile that equaled her curvy body. She had to be one of his Father's inamorata's.

"Are you looking for my Dad?"

"Yes, actually I am. Is he home?"

"Nope, he is out for the night."

The woman rolled her eyes indicating an irritation. "Then you will have to do."

A lapse in time he didn't remember must have occurred. Before he knew it, the slightly opened door was shut. She was standing in the living room glaring at the porno playing on the television. The woman turning towards him hearing the groaning on the tube. Darting her eyes up at Hagen, she snarled "You are a bit young for this, aren't you?"

"Maybe" He smiled with an embarrassment for his curiosity.

"I bet youngling, you are still a virgin."

The woman's wicked smile taunted Hagen. She was very attractive, but too aggressive. Hagen thinking sarcasm could help him out the humiliating situation, retorted "Okay, you found me out. Is there a purpose for your visit tonight? I told you my Dad wasn't home. Yet you are somehow in his house."

"Young, innocent, yet a smartass, you will be delicious for dessert."

The woman started licking her lips. Hagen knew she had just implied he was gonna be the dessert for whatever she'd eaten for dinner. He tried to gulp his anxiety down, but she invaded his space. Trying to wiggle away from the strange being, he backed away slowly. The woman grabbing his arm, asked again.

"Can you help me? It seems my vehicle has left me stranded from across the lake."

"You were across the lake? That is a long haul to walk around." Hagen stuttered while probing.

"Are you going to help me, or just ask questions?" Blowing the long bangs out of her eyes, she huffed.

"If I can, I will help you. I am young, remember?" Hagen answered with a touch of sarcasm to hide his fear from this beast of a woman.

"Follow me youngling." The woman tauntingly spoke making him freeze in a panic.

Things were getting strange with this woman. Directing his eyes to the floor, he soon realized she was wearing no shoes.

"Are you sure you walked all the way here?" blurted out of his frighten mouth.

The woman sashayed closer to Hagen. He wanted her to leave. She took his hands rubbing them across her plump breasts. Hagen's unpredictable hormones made his jeans tightened even more. It made the woman snicker.

"You wanna touch me." She said in a seducing but intimidating tone.

Hagen pushed her back, but she reentered his space. Insinuating another lewd suggestion, she shoved Hagen down on the couch. He

landed in a sitting position with this crazy female holding him down straddling his thighs. She gyrated herself down on his crotch. The situation scared him more than aroused him. He found the strength to throw her off him. Jumping up on his feet, he ran outside screaming. Feeling hands touch him, he yelled so loud his voice bounced off the trees. Black birds scattered into the dark skies. He knew by the laughter Noah and Sammy were at his rescue.

"Dude, what's wrong?"

Before Hagen could speak, they heard a rustling of the brush alongside the house prompting them to check out the cause of the noise. All the boys saw was a woman walking away from the house disappearing in the drifting fog.

"Scared of a little woman, Hagen?" Sammy snickered.

"Is she gone?" Hagen hysterically asked.

"Yeah, she ran to the woods. That's kinda freaky. What happened to make you all skittish?" Sammy laughed.

Hagen was gasping for breath from the frightening experience. Sammy kept on cracking jokes like a comedian with Noah as his audience. Frustrated, Hagen yelled, "Listen."

"It's not funny. The woman was crazy. She came here asking for my Dad claiming to be stranded. There was something off about her, very strange. Before I knew it, she was all over me. I think I wanna leave, go back to my Mom's house."

The cousins followed Hagen in the cottage. Sammy was older than Noah and him. He'd just graduated high school. Noah had celebrated his fourteenth birthday weeks ago. While Hagen still waited for the next month, becoming an official teenager. Sammy proceeded to taunt him opening the refrigerator door. He grabbed two beers tossing one to Noah, popping the cap on the other. Guzzling the carbonated alcohol down, Sammy wiped his lips grinning at him.

"I would offer you one, but if you can't even seduce a woman? You might want to not try the alcohol either." Sammy continued joking.

Hagen sat on the couch startled from the altercation. He felt Sammy's hand shuffle across from the couch patting his head like a dog.

"It's okay little cuz. She won't be back. If she does return, I will give her some Sammy shack." he chuckled.

"Sammy leave Hagen alone. Maybe the woman did attack him." Noah suggested. "Dude if some lady did that to me, I would so have tapped it. I surely wouldn't have been screaming out the door. You better grow up Hagen, you are in junior high now."

Hagen shook his head at the ignorance and arrogance of his horny cousins. He doubted that Noah had ever tapped anything but that beer he would regret drinking later. He had lied earlier about his sexual experience to his Dad. The truth was he had done nothing with anyone. The cousins couldn't even conceive that he had been attacked. Their dicks were doing all the thinking. Crossing his arms choosing to just shut up, Hagen again announced. "I think I am going to leave."

"Leave where? To go to your house? You are better off staying here. Your house is deeper in the woods, plus you have a real freak there. Ya know Denise. Look Dude, if what you say is true. It's more than likely strange Denise was playing a joke on you. The way you openly call her names. I wouldn't doubt if she sent one of her girls here to scare you." Sammy suggested.

"Yeah that's right. Anyways, we came here with a movie to watch. *Friday the 13th* should calm the nerves." Noah laughed.

The more Hagen thought about it, the more he found Sammy's analogy more than likely correct. It was the smartest thing that had come out of Sammy's mouth since arriving. Crazy Lezzy probably was behind it all. The boys all decided to hang out the rest of the night at Norman's cottage. After the movie, they all settled in to go to sleep. Hagen and Noah went to his room to sleep. Noah volunteered knowing he was still a little anxious. Sammy stayed on the couch to sleep yelling out, "I hope if she comes back, she finds me on the couch."

Rolling his eyes unamused, Hagen slammed his bedroom door. Secretly being thankful that Noah was sleeping on the floor near him.

Chapter Eleven

The empty seat in the truck reflected how lonely Norman's life was becoming. Hagen wanted him to go out for some fun. The truth was he didn't have a clue where fun was these days. Since the strange darling that strutted out of his house bare naked a few weeks ago, there was only work occupying his time. Driving through town with no plan, he decided to try out a new little diner that had just opened on the outskirts of town. It wasn't hard to find. The diner was built on a piece of land that was desolate. The sign flickered on and off giving it the full remote small town atmosphere. Norman parked his truck in the low lit dusty parking lot. He got out of his Ford chuckling, "This is how all the horror movies start, at a desolate restaurant on the edge of town."

He entered the establishment that had no bell on the door announcing his arrival. Only a cook from behind the counter yelling out, "Welcome, take a seat anywhere. A waitress will be with you soon."

Norman nodded his head finding a booth the farthest from the other patrons in a private corner. Flicking open the menu, the embarrassment of not being able to read settled in. This is when he missed Charlotte the most. She always read the menu to him. It was the trivial things that were reminders of the lost. At least Hagen came around supposedly taking care of him. But the fact was the boy couldn't cook. The meal he attempted to cook wasn't that appetizing. He'd thrown the burnt fish deep down in the trash when his boy had excused himself. It wasn't his boy's fault. Men weren't meant to cook. With Hagen's suggestion, the night events led to him sitting alone at a booth. Now starving at the isolated diner, with a menu he was unable to read. Beginning to feel sorry for himself, he was about to get up and leave when the waitress hurled out, "Norman Garret, is that you?"

The loud ringing voice from the stout woman startled him. She stopped beside him putting her thick hands on his shoulder, squeezing it with her long nails pinching through his shirt. Taking a good look at the husky woman realizing she was a blast from his past. A memory before Charlotte. "Could it really be her?" Norman thought staring for a moment. The girl he once knew had an athletic form to her body, but this woman was built like a man. The more he eyed her, it was obvious it was his ole flame Judy Broxton. Frozen in surprise, he sheepishly responded, "Hey."

The stout woman continued her booming introduction with a piercing giggle. "Norman, you know me. You used to know me well." She winked bumping his shoulder with her rolls of flesh.

Norman finally thawed enough from his shock to answer.

"Judy I would have never of recognized you, your giggle hasn't changed." He responded realizing the comment had not one compliment. Judy didn't seem to mind. She bent over clapping her hands in laughter.

"You are right Norman. Some things never change. What are you doing here? Where's the family?"

"They are all busy tonight." Norman sighed.

"Well if I was your wife, I wouldn't let a hunk of man like you out of my site." She giggled again.

Norman's blue eyes darted at her. She must have seen the sharp edge the words cut into him.

"Well, sadly she did. Charlotte and I are divorced now. She gladly released me from her site." Norman confessed.

The repetitive giggles ceased from Judy's overworking jaws. Her bubbly smile straightened to a serious display of sincerity conveying, "I'm sorry Norman. I know you loved your Charlotte. I heard the rumors. I didn't want to pry."

Norman closed his menu agreeing, "I did love my Charlotte. But she is not mine anymore. Life goes on as they say. Now, I am hungry. Do you have any suggestions?" he said with a gentle smile.

His smile made Judy's sunny spirit pucker up again giving charming complements. For a husky woman, she did have pretty eyes underneath the thick makeup she wore to try to take the focus off her body.

"Well Hun, we have some pot roast with potatoes and vegetables that is just to die for."

"Then bring me a plate of that with some sweet iced tea Miss Judy." Norman smiled.

118

"Sure thang, Sweetie." Judy hustled off to get his meal.

He watched her trample around trying to get back to him in record time. Judy's scooting and rushing made him laugh under his breath. The garment that she was wearing was hideous. It did nothing for her plump body. The uniform was pink with a white apron tied around her. The fake red rose pinned to her bouffant bleach blonde hair reminded him of the sitcom *Alice*. Judy even had the gum smacking to the side of her mouth like the character Flo did on the show. Her voice was loud and ungraceful too. The only difference was Judy was more than a couple of pounds heavier than the tall and lanky character. The cook yelled, "Order up" with Judy grabbing the plate filled with delicious smells while also carrying a cold glass of iced tea. She sat the meal down in front of Norman grinning, "I hope you like it Darling. Is there anything else you need?"

"Well I could use some company if ya got the time." Norman tried to hold in his snickers trying to say the words. It was obvious the woman wanted to sit with him. He didn't know how he composed himself when she responded looking at her watch announcing, "Well looky there? It's break time for me."

She plopped herself in the booth beside him. The swooshing sound of the seat almost made his sides bust in laughter.

Norman scooted a little away from her to give him room to eat. After getting comfortable, he started to talk as he ate.

"So, Judy you obviously know all about me. What about yourself?"

"Well, I am still Judy Broxton. I never married. I had fun, bunches of it. Then time caught up with me. The body changed, and now I am a waitress at this desolate diner. That's about it."

"You never married?" Norman asked with a bit of surprise in his voice.

"No. I never did. After you left me for Charlotte. I just made life fun, nothing serious. I guess there was never another you."

Norman continued to eat before responding. "I am not that good. Just have a conversation with Charlotte. You may be glad you got away." He suggested.

"I don't blame you. You married in a very strange family. They must have been cursed with all the bad luck that came their way."

Norman became choked on his food grabbing his iced tea to clear his throat.

"Darling you okay? I didn't mean to make you choke. I would never talk about the mother of your children, but you never had a chance. Her daddy was the town moonshiner. I hear her momma was kinda loose. Sorry, but I wasn't shocked. At least you survived."

In all honesty, he liked the way Judy looked at him. More of a victim than predator. A survivor more than a tyrant. She blamed him for nothing. He could sit here and talk to her all night. It was good for his wounded ego. Judy looking at her watch, a reminder that break was over. Before getting up she whispered, "I get off at eleven if you want to wait for me."

Norman grinned at the notion as she handed him the check. He paid for his meal leaving the diner. Getting in his truck, he had every intention of leaving. Glancing at his own watch, seeing it was a quarter till eleven.

121

Deciding to give ole Judy a thrill, he waited for her. Fifteen minutes later she came barreling out the restaurant looking around the dim lighted parking lot. Norman quietly got out of his truck approaching her from behind. He whispered in the shadows, "Looking for me?"

Judy twisted around so fast she almost knocked Norman down. Norman started to giggle at the insanity that he was giving her any time of day. There was something about her though, that was good for him. Implying she had to walk home, he waved his hand motioning her to the truck giving Judy a ride.

***

Judy unlocked the door to her home trampling in before Norman entered. She kicked things to the side that were in the path of the walkway to the table of stacked newspapers and magazines. Dropping her purse and keys down, while grabbing the clothes that laid across the couch. She threw them to the corner asking Norman to sit down. Shifting the bundled-up blanket to the side, he sat down immediately noticing the untidiness of her home. It hadn't been dusted in years it appeared. There were too many figurines and decorative hangings on the wall. Hangings that had cob webs formed at the ends of them. There were papers and mail everywhere. The dishes in the sink were filling the room with a stale odor, one of rotten scrambled eggs. She offered him some coffee giving him a mug that was stained. Not wanting to be rude, he sipped the coffee despite the gross cup. He felt a case of the chuckles coming back on at the craziness of the night. Judy didn't seem to mind that she invited him to her pig pen house. The situation entertained him. Norman didn't know it was about to get even better. The conversation between them is what kept him there. She thought highly of Mr. Norman Garret as she referred to him. He liked it too. Before he knew it, Judy had offered him a massage. She grabbed his hand to help him off the couch, plopping him in the lazy boy chair next to it. Judy went behind the chair as Norman felt her hands press on his shoulders. He tried to get up, but Judy linebacker held him down. The massage felt more like a man rubbing him down. Her hands were calloused and ruff. Not soft and dainty that he was used too. The uncomfortable rub down finally ended with her man muscles swiftly turning the chair straddling him. He gasped from the extra weight galloping his thighs. Barely being able to hold back his laughter of the encounter, he felt her huffing breath whisper in his ear, "I want you Norman."

Before deciding on the offer, Judy grabbed his cheeks forcing her tongue down his throat. After a few minutes of awkward kissing, she started caressing him revealing her sagging boobs attempting to seduce him. Norman felt the giggles emerging once again. He didn't want to hurt her feelings. She was making such an effort to please him. He guessed the invite was accepted, for he didn't resist when she carried him into the bedroom. She sat him on the bed while she undressed. He could see the imperfections of her body with every inch of cellulite. "God had been so unkind to her," he thought.

She continued to undress him with no skills on seduction. Norman felt like he was being disrobed by his mother. Laying back on her bed, he could smell the stale old sheets that made the atmosphere seem like a sleazy motel. Not being aware of how, but his cock was aroused. Maybe it was from the fan roaring in the corner that rotated wind across him. The aroma didn't much improve when she tumbled her leg across him adjusting herself on top. The aroma like the fish caught from the pond earlier invaded his nostrils. Norman didn't realize he was inside her chambers. Judy started slipping and sliding across him with moans coming from her throat. He couldn't hold the laughter in anymore. It came wailing out. Judy jiggled with every thrust, commenting how good his cock felt. It was the dirty talk that made him finally get off. Norman grunted at completion like the pig he'd have to admit being after this pathetic encounter. The aroma of rotting carcass became worse loosening her hold collapsing beside him. Through the awkwardness the laughter tried to invade his spirit once again. Oddly, this was the best night he'd had in a while. In a weird way, he enjoyed spending time with her and hadn't a clue to why. Maybe because she looked at him with clear eyes. Judy didn't know the monster he'd become. She made him feel like a super hero. A real man again. It was obvious she just wanted to please him. It was a long time since he had that. He felt superior over her, and it felt good.

"Judy may be the person needed for revamping himself." He thought grinning feeling her fingers caressing his dick.

Chapter Twelve

Carolyn Lewis rushed into the dwelling of her home in complete devastation. The visions of her husband having intimate relations with the secretary laid heavy on her broken heart. Being a witness was worse than death. At least if he had died, the memory of their love would still hold a purity in her mind. Losing him this way was more than she could carry. The Christian woman who never drank uncorked a bottle of wine, grabbing the largest crystal filling it to the top. Guzzling the alcoholic grapes down, the burn in her stomach made her finally break. Her wounded heart felt like shattering in a million pieces. She paced the floor back and forth with the wine glass in her hand. Shouting at the top of her lungs, "No. No. No." The tears flooded her pale cheeks, as snot gathered underneath her nostrils. When the wine glass became empty, she grabbed the bottle sliding down to her kitchen floor leaning against the cabinets. Sitting there for hours, her distraught mind fell to sleep with the consumption of the wine. Waking her from the movement of her husband leaning over, he took the bottle out of her hand. The question asked haunted her soul.

"What have you done Caroline?" he repeated several times. In solemn silence, Caroline stared unresponsive.

She tried to get up, but the spinning of the room made her sit back against the cabinet holding her head. Again, hearing the love of her life repeating the agonizing question once more.

"What have you done? You have never drank my love. What has brought this on? Did the ladies at life group commit blasphemy against God again with a little gossip?" he asked making a light joke of the situation.

Caroline lifted the empty wine bottle, throwing it across the kitchen. The bottle shattered into pieces hitting the wall.

"What have I done? You ask what I have done?" she abhorrently repeated.

Her hair looked teased from fiercely rubbing her hands through it. The tears fell from her eyes fast as the rapids streamed from a river. She started to beat the floor with her fists, cracking them. The blood came hurling out, but it didn't stop her. Ridge tried to grab her wrist to force her stop. She slipped her wrist quickly out of his hold, slapping him across the face.

Seeing the shock emerge in his eyes, he hadn't a clue to why she was acting such a way. Again, her husband of thirty- five years asked her, "What have you done for acting such way?"

Pointing to her chest screaming, "What have I done? It's never even occurred to you that the question you should be asking yourself is, what have you done?"

"I have been working. I've done nothing I am aware of. "He lied. "How I am to blame for this atrocious outburst?"

"You are a liar." she screamed.

Caroline slid up the cabinets holding on to the counter. Her voice was inaudible when she turned around and starting punching Ridge in the chest with her bloody hands staining his shirt.

He restrained her arms to stop the attack. With his strong hands around her wrists, she broke down and began to cry. Ridge still possessing the kind soul she had fell in love with, released her arms as she drifted into his chest asking, "Why?"

"Why? What? Tell me what you think I have done?"

Lifting her head with sorrowful eyes whispering, "I saw you. I saw you this afternoon with her. I saw you doing those things to her, with her."

Ridge slowly pushed himself away from her. The previous erratic behavior made him step away. Watching him wonder had she loaded the pistol in the safe, gave a weird gratification for his disloyal actions.

"I don't have the gun if that's what you are thinking. I haven't gone that crazy, not yet. I just want to know why. You are all I know. No man has ever touched me but you. I have been loyal and faithful. I just want to know why? How could you?" she asked with paused pants coming from her distraught voice.

129

She watched the man she loved all her life now pace the kitchen of their shattered life. Rubbing his hands through his sandy hair, the room went silent. Staring back at her, his reaction was something she had not expected. The apology was sincere. He was sorry, but not sorry for his actions. The justification of his behavior was more shocking.

"I don't know how you stand there asking me why? Darling, you know why. I may be the only man to have ever taken you. Yet no man has ever seen you completely naked. Lifting a flannel gown doesn't arouse a man. Did you ever once just want me. Yes, I have taken you. We have the kids to prove it. In thirty-five years, you have never completely given yourself to me. You never even desired too."

Caroline started to cry as Ridge invaded her space.

"It's gotta stop." She murmured.

"You want it to stop. Then give yourself to me. Right now, here on the counter or on the floor. For once let yourself go. Give yourself to me." He begged.

She felt him unbuttoning her shirt. With her bra exposed, he unclipped the clasp that was holding her boobs together. The moment she felt them exposed in bare air, her hands frantically closed her shirt. Caroline shivered stepping back from him.

"I can't do that. I am sorry." she cried.

"I'm sorry too." Ridge said with an unforeseen arrogance.

With no expression, he slowly sauntered out of the kitchen.

Carline devastated, slid back on the floor whispering, "What have I done?"

Chapter Thirteen

The softness of her tongue glided around his cock, taking on a whole new meaning of pleasure. His loins ached to release his juices. He moved his feet around while arching his neck. Lifting his eyes open. Sammy opened his eyes to the most memorable wet dream ever. It seemed so real. He squinted his eyes trying to focus when reality hit. It wasn't a dream. There she was. This beautiful woman Hagen had been rattled by between his legs, licking his cock like a lollipop. Her golden eyes were hypnotizing as Hagen described. "How did she get in here without making any kind of racket" he wondered, suddenly realizing he was completely bare to bone. He started to speak, but she signaled for silence. She slid like a snake up his chest. She held his arms from behind his head plunging down on his erect stick, slowly gyrating down until he was inside of her. Sammy was starting to understand Hagen's fear of the aggression of this mystical woman. The pleasure was intoxicating, but also wickedly terrifying. He tried to release himself from her hold. The tight thrusts made it impossible. He began to cum with her lifting herself off him. In an aroused fright, he watched her drink every squirt that came from the head of his cock. The left residue she smeared over her stomach like lotion. She stood up in front of him speaking in a whisper. "Be careful about what you wish for. You just might get it."

The woman silently walked across the floor like a spirit gliding out the door. Sammy jumped up to see where this weird creature was going. He watched in disbelief when the woman faded in the foggy darkness that surrounded the small home. Feeling a tingling burn, he glanced down at his penis seeing a marking on the top of it. He tried to rub it off, but it wouldn't even smudge. Running back inside panic stricken, he turned the lock dead bolting the door. Rushing into the bathroom turning on the faucet to the shower, he hopped in lathering the soap all over his body while scrubbing his cock. The marking was like a tattoo. It wasn't washing off.

"What the fuck." He yelled turning off the water. Yanking the shower curtain to the side he got out grabbing a towel off the rack. He dried his genitals still trying to rub the marking off. His heart raced thinking about the encounter that felt like rape. He knew he owed Hagen an apology for all the smart-ass jokes. Fear was overtaking his usual calm state. Forgetting about it was what he needed to do.

What could he say to Hagen anyways without sending his cousin into a nervous frenzy. He'd convinced his cousin to stay the rest of the night. Sammy decided to dress himself and pretend it never happened. It was the only logical thing to do.

He came out of the bathroom, returning to the living room. Plopping on the couch, he grabbed the remote. Going back to sleep after that wide awake nightmare wasn't an option. He relaxed his legs on the coffee table trying not to think of the experience. A sigh of relief emerged from his nervous stomach seeing headlights shine through the curtains. Relieved, his Uncle was home. Hearing the door unlock, Norman strolled in remarking, "Ya boys scared? Bolted in I see."

Sammy slightly smiled at the man he referred to as Uncle all his life. Since the divorce, he was of no relation. Even though when he was out with Norman and Hagen, few who did not know them would tell the three how much they favored. Often telling Hagen and him they looked like brothers not cousins. Still, Uncle Norman welcomed Noah and him over as if they were still his nephews. His uncle being home made his anxiety dissipate. If anything happened during the night, at least a mature adult would be there.

Norman opened the refrigerator door to grab a beer offering Sammy one. He had to admit he'd already helped himself earlier. Even being guilty of distributing alcohol to a minor when he had given one to Noah. Norman laughed at his admission, confiding "We all have given youth a sippy sip in our lifetime. Don't beat yourself up. Is that why you seem shaky? Afraid Lucie may find out?" he asked joining him sitting on the couch propping his legs up.

"That would be horrible." Sammy admitted. "But that is not what's got my nerves tangled. When we got here tonight Hagen was all freaked out. He wanted to go home. I had to convince him that being here was much better than being around strange Denise."

"Really? Hagen wanted to leave? That's unusual. He hates Lezzy, I mean Denise. I wonder what that's about." Norman pondered.

Sammy didn't want to tell his uncle about the strange woman. In fear he would not believe him. If that's what she even was. He didn't know himself anymore. Solace came surfacing

135

with Norman picking up the VHS off the coffee table.

"Well now it makes sense. I don't know why you boys watch these scary movies. Especially if they start out in desolate woods. *Friday the 13th* ? I see now why you boys are shaken. Hagen wants to be tough, but when it comes to these movies. He is still a boy." Norman laughed.

"Yeah I suppose." Sammy answered as he nibbled on his cuticles. Spitting them out the side of his mouth, he finally got the courage to tell Norman what was really bothering him.

"Uncle Norman, have you ever had any woman just show up here. Out of nowhere?"

Sipping the beer his uncle answered, "I don't believe I have."

Norman rested his arms on his chest before slamming his feet to the floor. He sat up straight remembering something alarming Sammy.

"Oh, but one time there was this woman. Believe it or not, she was ebony. A hot little thang I met at the bar. She had the softest skin, radiant eyes, and oh that ass. The woman just all but insisted that I take her home." Norman reminisced.

"So, did you bring her home?" Sammy curiously asked.

"Damn right I did. That honey couldn't even wait until she got me home. She blew me all the way here. When I pulled into my little cottage, she got out of the truck undressing. By the time she made it to the house she was naked and ready to go."

"What happened then?" Sammy continued to question.

Norman darted his eyes at the young man. Sammy knew his uncle thought he was a special kind of stupid.

"What do you think happened? I fucked her. It was the absolute best ass I have ever had. When we finished, she just left out of here ass naked. It was weird kinda."

"Weird? How can getting a piece of ass be weird?" Sammy asked hoping not to get the earlier reaction.

Norman lowering his voice scooted closer to him as if someone was listening to their conversation.

"Because she disappeared in the fog. She was just gone. I have never heard of or seen her since. I guess that is a certified one night stand." He chuckled with his arm bumping Sammy's.

Norman got up giving the boy a hug, slapping Sammy across the leg announcing he was going to bed.

Sammy grunted a "Good Night" as his uncle entered his room to retire for the night. A deafening boom came from outside that lit up the sky with radiating orange and red flames.

Sammy stood straight up with Norman returning to the living room. Hagen and Noah hustled from the bedroom joining them. With all four of them asking, "What the fuck was that?"

Chapter Fourteen

Rushing through the woods to get back home, Beatrice's feet kept tripping over the small brittle limbs that were hidden under all the brown crisp leaves. The note that she clinched in her hand had brought thrilling possibilities. She couldn't wait to get back home to make the call. One night in the mystical with Denise, she knew had brought her this good fortune. The wait for the audition was over. Her mind was reeling in anticipation of speaking to the band. The closer she got to home the mist of the evening fog was becoming denser. She could barely see her hands in front of her. Which made her even more clumsy with her feet. It felt like someone was right behind her. She kept turning to look but the fog made it impossible to see. The feeling of coolness touched her spine of her upper neck. Goose pimples formed all over her skin from the sudden whip of it. Looking over her shoulder again, there was nothing that she could see. The heaviness of being watched made her pace faster towards the house. Squinting her eyes, Beatrice reached her hands out to guide towards a clearing she could barely see. The coolness that had tingled her neck, had started to swirl around her body. It made her bones shiver. She started to twirl in a circle that made the clearing she could see disappear. Her once thrill turned into a dazed and confused state of mind. The images of dark souls swooshed around her body. She could feel hands trying to pull at her legs. Panic started to overtake her when she stumbled on another twig landing outside the dense fog into the clearing. Strangely she had landed on her hands and knees, looking up at her startled aunts. They were still standing in front of the bonfire she had left them at. Denise bent down to help her guide herself back to her feet.

"Humming Bird, are you okay? Did something frighten you?" Denise asked.

Beatrice jumped away from her aunt. The images of darkness still fresh in her mind. The coldness on her skin made her uncontrollably shake.

"I got turned around in the fog somehow. It's very thick once you go into the woods. I guess I got lost for a second." Beatrice said in a confused state.

"Sharon and I will help you get back. It's getting late. We should all get back before Charlotte returns." Denise said in a haste.

Beatrice trying to muddle her mind around what she had just experienced. Then realized her piece of paper with all her possibilities had dropped out of her hand in the confusion. She started yelling, "Oh no. I dropped my note." Collapsing to the ground on her knees, she scattered the leaves in hopes to find it. The note was nowhere to be found. She got back on her feet leaning forward to see if she had dropped her paper around the fire. It couldn't be there she knew. The tight hold she had on it before going into the woods. It was then she noticed the unusual circle around the fire. The curiosity of it engaged her attention. The energy that surrounded the circle was off. It consumed a wicked aura. The echoes of Denise's voice lifted her mind off the strange symbol.

"Here it is Humming Bird. Right where you landed." Her aunt said smiling noticing Beatrice was staring at the ground. Oddly, her aunt looked surprised about its circular appearance as she did.

Gazing up at Denise she asked, "What is this? Is it a symbol of evil? Does the magic you practice have darkness in it. Is the legend true?"

Beatrice gasped for air afraid to hear the answer.

That is when Sharon appeared slipping her arm around her to comfort her.

"No Darling, that is just foolishness your Granny came up with instead of having to deal with the truths of her own misfortunes. It's just a stupid legend. I just prayed with Denise. What she practices brings tranquility to the soul, to the earth. Don't worry your young brain about such things. Let's get you to the house before your Momma curses us all with foul language for having you out in the woods."

Beatrice walked hand in hand with both aunts. The woods were still foggy, but not as bad as before. She noticed Denise seemed edgy guiding them through the woods. She was speaking on how to never be afraid. The light of the moon would always lead you back from any journey. Her voice screeched like she was reminding herself of it as they jetted through the mist. The woods finally cleared to the opening of the house that shined of bright lights. They had made it back just in time seeing a car driving towards them. Aunt Lucie and Madeline jumped out of the car with Lucie hastily tromping toward them.

"What have yawl been doing? I saw you coming from the woods. What is going on here? Beatrice? Sharon?" Lucie questioned.

Beatrice watched as the normally close sisters had a battle of words between each other.

"Lucie, get the panties out of your crotch. We were just taking a night stroll." Sharon retorted.

"Panties in my crotch? Really Sharon? Since when do you talk to me like that? A night stroll? Sharon what has she done to you." Lucie asked pointing her finger in Denise's direction. "What has she done Beatrice?"

Beatrice wanted to shout out what had just happened in the woods, but in fear of Lucie telling her Momma she joined in with Sharon with the web of lies.

"Aunt Lucie we are okay. Don't you worry. We were just out walking. Sharon and Denise were talking, trying to reconnect. It was my idea to walk the trails Hagen has made throughout the woods. That's all."

Lucie stared into Beatrice eyes making her uncomfortable. Deep down she knew her aunt could feel the energy of her deceiving words.

"Lucie, I have not rubbed off any of the magic or gayness on Humming Bird." Denise announced in a condescending tone.

"Humming Bird?" Lucie asked. "Since when do we call Bee Humming Bird?"

"It's a sweet name I call her because of her amazing voice. Is there something wrong with that?" Denise lashed back.

Beatrice could see in all her aunt's eyes, they wanted to tear each other apart. How did her night of just wanting to call the band back turn into this? From the corner of her eye she could see Madeline standing beside Lucie's car. She had been so quiet Beatrice had forgotten she was there. Madeline kept staring up at the sky. It looked as though she was expecting something. The arguing diverted her attention back on her aunts hearing Sharon yell, "Lucie, don't be such a paranoid freak."

Lucie and Sharon were yelling in each other's faces when Beatrice heard her sister scream.

The thundering boom rang throughout the woods for miles. Beatrice ran to Maddie seeing the fire in the sky. The illuminating flames brought silence to everyone. Beatrice started to shake seeing the power of the explosion. She felt like a little girl wanting her mother. A sigh of relief came seeing her Momma arrive home. Momma hurried out of the car with a frantic tone rushing them to get in.

"That explosion is near Norman's house. Get in. Hagen is there." Momma shouted.

"Oh Lord. I think Noah and Sammy are there too." Lucie rushed to the car signaling Beatrice to get Maddie to their Momma's car.

Sharon jumped into her own vehicle with Denise joining her. Beatrice watched the headlights bump up and down from Sharon's car as they all sped out of the woods. Lucie was nervously babbling to her mother in the front seat. She was doing her usual blaming Denise's presence in their lives for all the strange occurrence's. The closer they drove to her Father's place, it was apparent something had blown up near there. Remembering her own creepy occurrence earlier in the evening, Beatrice had a very awful feeling something

had just happened. She dreaded finding out
the answer.

Chapter Fifteen

Running through the woods the smoke from the fire became thick. Norman and the boys tried to see where the explosion had come from. They ran near across the other side of the lake when the sound of scuffles came from the sudden stop. Norman could see the truck blazing with fire. The gas tank had exploded catching some of the trees on fire. It appeared that the truck also had diesel fuel kept in the back of it making the explosion even greater. The fuel had leaked around an already built bonfire that inflamed the top of the lake. Getting closer to the area, he discovered a scene nothing could have prepared him for. The gruesome site of two dead men. In the shock of it, he realized they were not dead before the explosion. They laid by the bank of the lake fully naked. One laying with his chest to the dirt, with the other on top of him. Norman stopped the boys before they went any further. The sight sickened him. It was obviously queers had been discovered by someone. Who then viciously murdered them. The boys tried to proceed forward but Norman turned around yelling, "Stop. Stay there."

He stepped slowly toward the bodies not knowing if whoever had done this still lurked in the smoky darkness. Looking around his perimeter, seeing everything was clear glimpsing at the burning truck again. He took another look shaking his head thinking, "Nah."

The closer he got to the horrific scene the gorier it became. The heads of the men were gone. Whoever tortured to the poor souls somehow had torn their heads off. There was so much blood, Norman bent over beginning to puke. He noticed the man's hand. Wiping the vile off his mouth, he didn't want to look but he forced himself too. Studying the man's hand, he realized the hand resembled his own. Shaking his head again in disbelief, he rushed to the side remembering the tattoo his brother had gotten years ago. He had teased his brother it was for homosexuals with the barbed wire of roses intertwined around the muscle of his upper arm. The reality hit when he saw the same ink on the dead man's arm. Norman glanced back at the truck knowing it was his brother Bobby's. In an instant, he knew the other man had to be Dan. Falling to his knees he started to scream with the agony of the reveal. His screams brought the boys to the area. Norman tried to keep Noah away, but the boy ran screaming already finding his Dad's tackle box from the place he had made the boys wait. Watching the young man scream, the shocking site made Norman come back from his own grief. Knowing he had to get

Noah away from bloody scene, he dragged the boy as he screamed holding his arms out gripping his fist. Sammy and Hagen wasn't doing much better. Sammy tried to hide his tears, while Hagen put his hands over his eyes hollering, "Oh God."

Taking control Norman shouted, "Sammy run ahead of me and call for help. Hagen, you go too. I will be behind you carrying Noah. C'mon let's go."

It was the longest run ever. Norman held Noah in his arms like a newborn baby. The young man crying inconsolable tears holding on to Norman's shoulder's unable to walk. Every other second, he would see Sammy look over his shoulder with appalled glares making sure they were all secured together.

Images of the horrific scene reeled through his shocked mind trying to get home without dropping Noah. The fire, the blood, and the sexual position the men were in. He had known his brother all his life. There was no way in hell the man was gay. Neither was Dan. Someone had done this to them. Someone evil. Or maybe even worse, something evil. Damn he didn't want to sound like Lucie. How could this be explained? His heart hurt too much right now to grasp it. He had lost his best friend, and his brother. With every step holding Noah, Norman's own mind was starting to race. Knowing he had to keep it together, he felt some relief seeing the clearing to his house. Sammy hustled to get to the front door with Hagen behind him. It was only a few seconds, Norman arrived with Noah placing the distraught boy on the couch. He could hear Sammy's voice resonating anxiety speaking to the sheriff on the phone. Hearing the phone hang up, Norman stood in silence as Sammy and Hagen paced the floor. Sammy kept screaming, "What the fuck happened? What the fuck?"

Norman tried to calm the boys down knowing he was also about to lose it too. He felt his knees buckling with excruciating pains coming from his abdomen. The scene would be engraved in his head for eternity. How could he get through this? He started to cry sliding his hand through his thick hair. The sound of the sirens made his temples feel like they were going to explode. Soon his yard was covered with the sheriff and the fire department. Sammy ran out the door instructing them where to go. That's when dread consumed him hearing one officer say, "Is your Uncle inside?"

The man stood before him asking what he knew. Which was nothing. They were instructed to stay put. The fire rescue hustled to fight the blaze, while the sheriff department investigated the scene.

Figuring at some point he would have to call Lucie and Sharon, Norman finally broke. He couldn't handle this alone. Hagen came over to console his Dad while Sammy stayed with Noah. The scene rolled through his mind like a projector in slow motion. He exhaled a deep breath remembering it. At that moment, he wanted the comfort of Charlotte. Hearing Hagen's voice echo, "Do you want me to call Momma?" His head nodded forward giving his son the go ahead. Everything was rotating around him like he was on some drug induced trip. Except he was sober seeing, feeling it all. His anxiety had reached its breaking point when the door swung open with Charlotte rushing into his arms in distraught asking, "Where's Hagen?"

Chapter Sixteen

Staying behind at a distance, her sisters rushed
inside the home of her once brother in law.
Denise studied the area breathing the remnants
of the Goddess. She suspected Amora was near
having observed the circle earlier. Being fooled
by the trance, she thought her own mystical
ability had invaded Sharon. It was the
phantom of her lover all along. Glancing
around at this disaster, the questions rotated in
Denise's head. "What had Amora done? Why
was she sabotaging all her work?" It had taken
her weeks to get this close to the family. The
interference angered her. Hearing the screams
coming from the entrance of the home
confirmed all her suspicions. Not knowing
what to do she just glared at her surroundings
watching Beatrice running to join the others.
Leaving Madeline alone with her, she felt small
fingers tug at her arm. Detecting the young
girl was startled by the commotion, Denise
bent to her knees peering into Madeline eyes.
She could see much bravery behind her baby
blues. The girl's soul was strong, more
courageous than any she had ever
encountered. Because inside this strong
courageous soul was a purity she had never
felt. The youngling began to speak knowing

Denise was involved in this destruction somehow.

"Is this like home to you." Madeline boldly asked.

"Home? I don't understand? Elaborate." Denise answered trying to get into her niece's mind.

"Elaborate?" the girl curiously asked. "What does that mean?

"More details sweet one." Denise sarcastically retorted.

"Oh. I don't want to seem rude. This is me elaborate what I see."

Denise couldn't help but genuinely laugh this time. The girls had a sweetness to her. It was captivating. Madeline's peaceful energy was strange to her dark soul.

"Sweet one, you now are elaborating." She corrected.

"Auntie you are not taking me seriously. I am used to it. Nobody does but listen. Is your home in the woods of Georgia like the inferno that is destroying everything here? Fire destroys. You don't fool me. I see the flames deep in your pupils. You live in darkness with raging fires. Is this destruction yours?"

Denise usually quick to respond was diverted by the deepness of the question. Madeline continued to grind the interrogation of her intentions.

"Don't try to deny it. I see the flames in your eyes like I did with the man. I will be watching you as you have been sent here to watch me. I don't fear you." Madeline inquired, daring for a girl of her age.

"Furthermore, what you don't know is all is not lost. Not even your soul until the final breath has been taken. You have been deceived. I will pray for you even with the knowledge that you seek to destroy my family."

"Sweet one why would you say such things to me? I mean no harm to your family." Denise said trying to disguise whatever the girl was visioning.

The girl leaned in closer to her determined to get her point across.

"Even as the fire burns in you, I will pray for you. It doesn't have to be this way Auntie. I will not let you harm my family. I will be watching you."

Denise staggered by her intuitive visions but silenced by young soul's body language. She with the audacity to curl her perfect eye brows downward indicating a direct statement that she had been warned of the damnation of God.

Hearing the calls from Hagen's voice, bellowing for his youngest sister's whereabouts. Madeline waved her hand running towards her brother, but not before she turned around raising those eyebrows at her again.

Denise's maleficent aura was taken by surprise by Madeline's admissions. The love that evolved from the girl's soul made her feel vulnerable. An emotion that hadn't entered her body in years. She felt compelled to talk more to the girl. Shaking her head returning to her blackened heart, she thought for a moment the girl made a scratch in her cold icy heart. The feeling she needed to rid herself of. Standing up straight to take control of herself, she marched towards the house to discover what the Goddess had destroyed.

***

The site of the sheriff bringing the bodies to the coroner's van was a devastating sight for the family. The body bags were zipped up and covered, but Denise could feel the men had no heads. The sheriff department finally let the family, at least the adults come to the scene. Beatrice and Sammy stayed back at the house caring for the younger ones. Norman guided everyone through the woods, as Charlotte comforted Lucie. Denise put her arm around distraught Sharon who was inconsolable with tears gushing down her face. They all entered the opening of the smoke-filled scene. Ash was still trickling down like snowflakes from the fire that had been put out. The torched truck made the reality of the scene become very real. The moon shined a bright orange that kept the area somewhat lit. It was like mother earth knew the evil that had roamed the area. Sharon screamed out at the sight of the bloodstained dirt. Denise held her tight whispering in her ear, "Mother of the night, give this soul peace."

Staring straight into her sister's eyes, Denise was reminded of the earlier peace she felt praying. Sharon slowly moved away from her, walking toward the smoggy lake. She watched as her sister prayed, but to which power she did not know. It came to her mind that the Goddess could be invading her soul once again. It confused her. Looking over everything, the evidence was conclusive. The headless men, the fire, and the circle that surrounded the sight. This was the work of Amora. "Why would she do this?" repeated in Denise's mind over and over.

While observing everything trying to gather it all in her mind, the disgruntled wrath of Lucie's voice descended upon her direction.

"You did this. You witch." Lucie screamed.

Denise startled, backed away as Charlotte tried to stop her. Lucie pulled away from their sister, charging straight for her. Lucie hands wrapped around Denise's neck, pushing her to the ground with a slick kick of her feet. Lucie's tight grip made Denise start choking before Norman and the sheriff ripped the woman off her. Denise immediately turned to her side gasping for air.

"Stop it." The men yelled with the sheriff adding if it didn't cease, he would be hauling somebody to jail.

Lucie would not stop with her tirade. Her blood curdling screams and hollering didn't halt until she started hyperventilating. Charlotte assisted trying to calm and quiet her. The accusations continued towards Denise.

Denise arose to sitting on her knees still wheezing from the attack. The stout sheriff with a deep voice went to her defense announcing the crime was an act of hate that ended in murder. He proceeded to inform the family in a subtle tone. That the investigation was leaning towards this conclusion with all the evidence they had available. He told the tale of how the two men were engaging in sexual activity when someone came upon them. The unsub tortured, then killed them in a ritualistic way. He gave the distinct detail of both men having what appeared to be a pentagram engraved on the top of their penis. He ended the horrid speech announcing to the family, "I am so sorry I had to tell you this. It's better to come from me than anyone else."

Denise gazed up rubbing her neck watching Norman lose his composure for a moment. He pleaded asking the sheriff to not release the details of sexual activity. She heard him say, "Just say they were fishing." The sheriff having compassion agreed. But warned if the suspect was caught, he may not be able to keep those details sealed. The anguished man she thought was a disaster, for a moment she felt the feelings of sorrow for him. What he didn't know is the men were just fishing. The vision told her so. It also told her Amora had approached them. They had no interests in a sexual encounter with her. Maybe that is why they came upon her wrath. It had angered her. Is that why she marked them? Usually the mark was for the sin of lust or incest. The mark signified the soul was destined to be devoured by the horn one. Eventually they would meet their fate. Once marked, the soul's fate was sealed.

The words the sheriff delivered only added salt to the family's deep wounds. Charlotte helped get Lucie back to the cottage with Norman following. Sharon was still standing at the lake. She hadn't screamed out or cried since arriving

159

there. Denise slowly trudged over to her. Sharon turned around with hatred taking the place of her grief.

"I knew the bastard was fooling around. I didn't know it was with a man. So much for the makeover."

Denise didn't know what to say. She couldn't blow her cover revealing what had really happened. Fully aware she needed to stay focused on her mission, she decided to keep quiet until she could summon the Goddess for answers.

Chapter Seventeen

Father Carson finished drying the last dish
from the earlier dinner. Wiping the plate until
it shined, he opened the cupboard carefully
placing the china in its rightful place. Not
being able to get the vision of the angel out of
his mind, he hung the dish towel on the handle
of the refrigerator. Then proceeded to the
garden for his nightly meditation. Upon
entering, he admired the stars flickering from
the heavens giving enough light to see the
beautiful images of his outside sanctuary. The
red roses were dearest to his heart, but the
smell of the lavender made the surroundings
peaceful. After taking in the tranquility of the
trickling water that flowed from the fountain,
he sat on a stone bench clearing his thoughts
for meditation. The images of the angel's
powerful magnificence lingered in his
memory. To meditate one must empty the
mind, but the task became impossible with
what he had witnessed earlier. Deciding to
pray he began to speak aloud knowing no one
could hear but the Lord and himself. The
lonely confinement was his punishment for his
sin.

"O Lord, Jesus Christ, Redeemer, and Savior,
forgive my sins. Count not my transgressions, but

rather my tears of repentance. Remember not my iniquities, but my sorrow for the offenses I have committed against my Father."

Before he could say, "Amen." The rustling of the brush diverted his attention. Moving his head around to see nothing, he attempted to continue when a spark of light illuminated to the side. As he glanced over his shoulder, the view of the magnificent angel sitting beside him caused an overwhelming feeling of tenderness. Dropping to his knees once again, he heard a subtle soft voice speak.

"Thank you, but please take your seat. I am the admiral of our Father's army, but I don't need to be bowed upon every time I appear to you."

Father Carson eyes were mesmerized by the angel's existence. If there was any doubt in his holiness, all ceased seeing the powerful angel dressed in armor with his mighty silver sword hanging from his side. The angel spoke again with the him continuing to listen.

"I am Michael. I guess you already know that. I heard you speak to the girl's aunt tonight. What you have heard is true. Pure souls are being born to the earth. As you figured,

Madeline is one of the chosen souls. That is why I am here, to protect her."

Father Carson was at a loss of words. He had prayed to the angel a many of days. Now he was sitting beside him. He could feel his tongue turning in knots answering the almighty being.

"I thank you Saint Michael. There is much evil after the young soul. She will need your holy protection."

The angel held the priests by his hand. His deep blue eyes staring straight into his soul. Father Carson could feel his righteous love for the girl through his gaze.

"Do not just thank me. Do your part. You pray to our Father every day for forgiveness. You should know you were forgiven decades ago, yet you still ask?"

"There is much I need to be forgiven for. You ask me to do my part? I don't understand. What can I do?" Father Carson humbly asked.

"You must go to your daughter if she does not come to you. You must pray. If they invade her body, you must perform an exorcism for her soul." The angel informed.

Father Carson leaned back stretching his back, squeezing the angel's hand tight. He paused taking a deep breath before speaking.

"I cannot leave this sanctuary." Father Carson stuttered back.

Michael gripped his hand tighter to keep the fear from invading his body. The priest felt peaceful by the hold. Michael was asking him to leave the very place that had kept him safe all these years.

"If you trust in our Father, you will find the strength. Do you not believe what you confess from your mouth daily?" Michael scolded.

"I do. But I sinned. Twice I committed the same sin. I can't even tell my daughters' the truth."

"Then it is not Father's forgiveness you seek. Father forgave you the moment you asked. The forgiveness you seek is from within. Only you can do that. Your daughters need you now. You took the wicked out of one daughter's soul. You are strong. The love for your daughters has given the once broken man back his strength."

Father Carson began to shake falling to his knees still griping on to Michael's hand.

"I succeeded in taking the darkness from her. I am thankful for that. I know how the evil works. It will try to lure me again. I fear that."

Michael stood up towering over the kneeling priest. His hand loosened the grip to a comforting hold.

"You are human, Father Carson. You may have failed Lilith, but all is not lost. You can protect your flesh and blood. Part of your goodness is in the pureness that went into Madeline. Be strong. The only power the dark forces can conquer is your own self-doubt and fear. Forgive yourself."

The tears flowed from the priest's weary eyes. It had been many years since he felt free from the bondage of the curse. Michael had given his strength back. Leaning his head into the palm of the angel's hand, Father Carson promised, "I will Saint Michael."

Michael's wings flapped out in glorious view. Father Carson watched as the admiral in the Lords army nodded his head downward towards him. The angel hurtled up disappearing in the star-studded skies.

Father Carson sat back on the stone bench to take in all that had happened. After a few minutes, he left his outside sanctuary to return to his quarters. The locked doors to the Cathedral rumbled with aggressive pounding. The loud banging became more repetitive. He frantically unlocked the door finding Lucie distraught rushing in. "Help me." She pleaded before collapsing in his arms.

Chapter Eighteen

Denise finished her cup of coffee in deep thought. Charlotte's soft lips kissed her on top of her forehead. Along with receiving a gentle hug from her sister before retiring to bed. It had been a peaceful day to end in such an exhausting hostile way. She was thankful it was over. Before her sister exited the kitchen, she reminded her, "It wasn't your fault. Don't let what Lucie said get to you. She just needs to blame someone for things we do not understand. I love you, Sis. I am glad you are here."

"Me too." Denise struggled to say.

Sitting at the table for a few more minutes to absorb all the day's events, it confused the hell out of her. She was sent to this place with a mission. A mission now being invaded upon by the commander. Denise got up gliding across the kitchen into the living room. Peeking down the hallway to make sure everyone was asleep, she could hear her nephew's snoring rippling down the hallway. He had come home bringing Noah with him. She guessed he needed the comfort of his Mother after the horrible scene he'd witnessed.

Tonight, she didn't feel much like calling him the troll. He was just a boy who had been traumatized in the worse of ways. Witnessing his compassion for Noah made her heart flutter once more like it did earlier in the night. With even volunteering to take the couch, so her nephews could rest comfortably. These are things that usually meant nothing to her cold soul. The emotions were strange to her. Compassion is something that didn't exist within her. Since being in the Florida woods with her sister, all these weird feelings were stirring like a cauldron of stone soup. A recipe she learned many years ago. The recipe was just throwing in all different kinds of ingredients not knowing the outcome. It could be something wonderful, or something disastrous.   Maybe her sentiments were changing from the closeness between the family. Nothing seemed to come between Charlotte and her crew. Her sister forgiving the man who had abused her confused Denise. Her mind needed to refocus on just the mission. Slipping her feet into her flip flops, she slowly opened the creaking front door to exit the home. Sneaking out, she vanished into the dark hazy woods. Bowing to the moon, she called out for the Goddess.

"Goddess of the night, bless me with images of your mystical being." She chanted.

A shadow figure circled her body in the misty haze. Knowing her love was there, feeling her invisible fingers slipping inside her gown. Her head bobbed back not able to fight the sensation. Amora appeared in front of her caressing her nipples.

"More." She groaned feeling the euphoria of her hands cup around her breasts.

Lifting her head forward to face her Goddess, a hard-whipping slash slit across her beautiful face. In the moment of confusion, she screamed "Amora."

The dagger the Goddess held slashed down her gown tearing it open. Denise found herself being knocked to the ground for the second time that night. Amora straddling her legs, plunged the dagger up her cervix without cutting her. Denise's heart raced feeling its sharpness invade her insides.

"What have I done, my love?" she pleaded.

Amora's enchanting eyes turned red with flickering fire raging from her pupils. Denise knew saying one wrong word, the Goddess would could cut her from the vulva to her throat.

"Did you think I would not feel your compassion for the souls. The putrid stench of the flutter in your heart. It sickens me."

"I don't understand what I feel? Please Amora, I came tonight to ask you how to rid me of these feelings." Denise begged.

Amora leaning in closer to intimidate her, still holding the dagger up her vagina.

"You came tonight to question me. Do you think I am a fool? You do not question the Goddess of the night. For if you do, you are the fool." Amora declared gritting her teeth that resembled fangs showing her true self.

"I do not question. I don't understand. Help me." Denise begged.

"You need not to understand. You just need to obey me. Do we understand each other?"

Amora threatened slicing a nick across her delicate clitoris. The sharpness of the dagger stung deep. Denise buckled her knees in the painful agony. Amora seizing the front of her face with the tongue of a snake slithering across the bloody slit inflicted on her cheek. The Goddess enraged demanded, "Do we understand each other?"

"Yes, my Love. I understand. Please forgive any trespass I have committed against you." Denise's voice shrieked with fear.

Feeling the dagger slide out of her insides, Amora guided her head in between her legs inserting one finger inside her. Exiting with blood on the tip of her nail from the wound, she licked it.

"Good girl." The Goddess replied patting her mound.

Denise cleared her mind to protect herself. The Goddess invaded her temple again, plunging her tongue inside her chambers. The power of the vigorous licking made her climax within seconds. Amora lifted herself off Denise, standing directly in front of her.

"Next time inamorata, there will be no punishment. Don't under estimate me, your soul belongs to me. I will kill you." The Goddess threatened before vanishing leaving a haunting wind that rustled the leaves on the ground.

Denise sat up on her knees. Afraid to think knowing Amora knew her every thought, she began to cry. Looking at her shredded gown was a reminder of how she had been deceived. Fearing to have any kind of thought fluttering through her mind, she stared blank into the darkness of the skies. A shooting star grabbed her attention gliding across the black smoky sky. The flickering light descended from above to the front of her feet. The light reflected the image of an angel. Stunned, she backed away with an unexpected modesty that had her closing the opening of her cut gown.

"Do not fear me. I bring you no harm." He instructed.

Immediately realizing that the image was a mighty Angel standing before her, she began to uncontrollably shake. They angel's eyes pierced blue that commanded his powerful abilities.

"Why are you here? You must go. The Goddess will know you are here. She will kill us both."

The angel slightly smirked. "She cannot cause any harm to me. You have been deceived."

"But she can to me. Please go. She probably already feels you. I must go."

Denise jumped to her feet proceeding to rush around the angel in a haste. He gently grabbed her arm. Glaring up, she gazed into his beautiful blue eyes. The goodness he carried was overwhelming. She turned her eyes away to not feel it.

"Yes, she can kill you." He agreed in a serious manner. "Don't fear her. I have strengths she can't break nor destroy. She cannot feel me with you here. For I have protected you."

The bones in Denise's body rattled hearing the words of the angel. Tears followed gushing down her delicate cheeks.

"Why would you protect me? I am the destroyer. I came here with a mission of destruction." Denise asked with anguish.

"I am Michael. The protector of souls. You are still Father's child. He felt your compassion. That is what brought me here. To give you the help your heart asked to receive. I trust you will now help protect the soul you came to destroy."

"How can you be sure that I am trust worthy." She questioned staring at the magnificent admiral.

"Because Father felt what's in your heart. I have been informed. There is no Goddess mightier than the Father. Lucifer my brother knows this. My power protects you. They will not be able to invade your being." Michael conveyed.

Turning her eyes back into his made her want him in a way she had never wanted a man. It was the first time she experienced pure compassion. The love from it aroused her. She leaned in closer to the angel touching his muscular pecks that were shielded in armor. Her arms glided across his neck lifting her leg to stroke his thigh. She felt his tender hand stop her further foundling.

"Control yourself." He executed.

She continued the seduction, but he pulled away commanding, "Stop. This is not the only way to love. Love has nothing to do with the flesh, it's about the soul. Give your love to Father and you can fight your earthly temple. You must do so for me to protect you. The lust will guide you back to the darkness. I can protect you, but only one can protect them from themselves. You must understand this."

Denise hung her head with embarrassment. Another emotion she hadn't felt in some time.

"Father says don't feel ashamed. This is new to you." The angel encouraged.

"Yes, it is. I feel strange."

"You understand what the wicked is attempting to accomplish. They desire Madeline's pureness of her soul. Amora wants to be powerful. Lucifer wants to destroy the girl in an attempt to defeat heaven. We must protect her together." He confided.

Denise walked to the tree that hung over them. Her hands glided around the tree wanting to believe the peace that she practiced still existed. Mother earth was not wicked. The trunk of the tree was rigid on her finger tips. She inhaled the smell of the bark of the giant oak. How could her peaceful beliefs about the earth be tied into the wicked. The angel gently placed his hand her shoulder. She turned around confessing, "Don't touch me. It's confusing. I still have lust I haven't taken full control of. As for Madeline, I will try to protect her. The purity of goodness shines bright in her eyes much like yours."

The angel so graciously bowed thanking her. His words gave her the peace she needed.

"You do not have to change your peace with the earth. Father encourages it. You can still practice as a diversion to the evil. Your work won't damn the soul for you are a soldier for our kingdom now."

Confused she asked, "Why does the Father or you need me to help protect her?"

"Because we can't interfere with free will. Charlotte unbelieving in the darkness puts her soul in danger. Madeline has deep love for her mother. Do you understand?"

Denise gasped. All was coming clear to her now. This answered why she couldn't focus on the angel when she knew he spoke to Madeline. He was much stronger than any evil. His words gave her the knowledge of how the enemy slithers into the cracks of their mighty foundation. Knowing this information, she could use it to terminate the girl. The recollection of how easy her once love turned on her removed any once loyalty. Amora had never really loved her. The Father who should have no mercy on her soul had sent the angel. The power of his love made her want to destroy her once Goddess. It wouldn't even be the work of revenge or karma. The path would be Father's will.

With a divine aura surrounding her, Denise took Michael's hand gently kissing the palm. She returned the bow to him promising, "I will protect her with all my being."

Chapter Nineteen

A troubling feeling emerged from his gut watching his mother drive away from his uncle's house. Sammy had offered to go home with her, but she insisted he stay with Norman. The expression on her face made it clear she wanted to be alone. Her isolation worried him. For reasons unknown, his mother's behavior had been off for weeks. This could be potentially detrimental to her. Rubbing his eyes from the stress of the evening, he turned around seeing Norman quietly sitting on the couch. Realizing his uncle was in immense agony, Sammy joined him on the couch. Not knowing what to say, he glided his fingers along the cushion of the blue flower design on the colorful couch. Powering his eyes back up he noticed the tear drops lightly dripping from Norman's eyes. It pained him watching this strong man breathe in, slowly breathing out from pure shock. Sammy made the conscience decision to remain silent until his uncle spoke. The hour passed by hearing the crickets chirp from outside. They seemed to stay in rhythm with the ticking of the clock that hung on the wall above the television. The mourning doves sang a caroling tune of eerily coos. Their calls of warning of the evil that still graced the woods. It sent chills to his skin. The only good came when their invasive tweets finally broke the deafening silence.

"Even the birds know something is off tonight." Norman commented.

Sammy jumped at the sudden unexpected speech. Taking his eyes off the white ceiling he had stared at for over sixty minutes, he twitched around adjusting himself on the couch.

"The whole night has been weird. I can vouch for that. First Hagen being scared out of his mind, the woman, and now all this shit. My head can't seem to wrap around it all." Sammy blurted.

Norman's back lifted sitting straight up. Sammy tilted his head back knowing the bursting of words opened a can of worms. His intuition knew the question to be asked."

"What woman? You never said anything about a woman?" his uncle proceeded to interrogate.

Sammy stretched his arms up with his legs held outward before settling back into sitting position. Before the conversation began the thought of the woman made him shudder. His uncle examining with his eyes asked, "You alright Sammy?"

Sammy felt himself spring up from the couch. His nerves had the better of him making the decision earlier not to remember the event. Now he had too, especially after seeing Dan and Bobby. Their nude headless bodies. The blood still gushing fresh in his mind. The stench of the bodies. He never knew death had a distinctive smell. The one thing that troubled him the most was the sheriff telling of the marking that was engraved on their penis. It was much described like the one he now had on his own. It terrified him. He started to pace when he heard Norman asked again, "You alright?"

"No, Uncle Norman I am not." He confided stuttering. Taking a breath, he began to speak.

"Tonight, when Noah and I arrived here. Hagen was running toward us hysterical. He was babbling about a woman being inside. I didn't really know what to think about it, but he mentioned she was aggressive towards him. I saw a woman disappearing in the fog. But I really thought he was exaggerating. Wow was he so not exaggerating. We watched a movie, Noah went to Hagen's room to sleep so he wouldn't be scared. I took the couch. I woke up to this beautiful woman between my legs giving me the best blow job I've ever had. She got aggressive with me. Not in a good kind of way either. I found myself terrified. Afterwards she just floated like a ghost disappearing out in the fog. That is when I noticed it."

Sammy paused his words for a few moments still pacing the floor with his hands holding the back of his neck. He plopped back down on the couch with fear consuming him. Figuring his uncle wound never believe him, he blurted out his terror.

"I have the same marking on my penis that the sheriff described. You are right Uncle Norman. Something is terribly wrong tonight. I think the markings may mean something. I think I am next." Sammy exclaimed.

Sammy couldn't look at his uncle afraid he didn't believe his confession. His uncle grabbed his shoulders shouting, "Look at me Sammy. Calm down. Describe the woman?"

"Skin like honey," Sammy began to say when his uncle joined in. "Eyes of gold, dark long hair, luscious bronze lips."

Sammy saw his fear transfer onto Norman's face. He felt the pounding in his chest. Seeing his uncle's breath, he knew his heart was racing too.

"You have the marking too?" he asked shivering.

"Yeah, I do. Until tonight I choose not to think about it." Norman admitted.

"What does it mean? Are the stories of the Piney Woods true? Is Aunt Lucie right?" Sammy asked with exasperation.

"I don't know but when morning breaks, we are going to find out some answers." His uncle assured.

***

Sammy woke to the sunlight peeking around the curtains blinding his focus. It amazed him he could nod off on the couch to a deep sleep after all was revealed. Glancing over to see if Norman was sleeping, he realized his uncle was gone. Sammy stumbled to his knees feeling the aches in his legs. Staggering to the bathroom, he lifted the toilet lid to relieve himself. The marking was sore on the top of his penis. The more he stared at it, the more he wanted to know what it meant. Flicking his dick, he adjusted himself back inside his jeans. Turning the water on from the faucet, he picked up the bar of soap that laid by the sink to wash his hands. Peering into the mirror, he thought he saw he saw something behind him. When he turned his head to check a hand plunged from the mirror with long brown hairy fingers wrapping around his throat. From his peripheral vision the image of a demonic goat headed creature reflected. Feeling the tight grip around his throat was making it difficult to breath. The only thought he had was God help me. The moment the thought ran through his mind, the being turned him loose. He fell to the bathroom floor hearing glass shattering from the mirror. All Sammy could focus on was getting out of the house. Still out of breath, he lifted himself up, stumbling through the living room running out of the home. His screams echoed the woods that summoned Norman who was out looking around the property. Seeing his uncle sprinting in a mad dash, Sammy felt a sigh of relief.

"What's wrong. Why are you hollering?"
Norman asked huffing for breath.

"Something grabbed me in the bathroom from
the mirror?" He frantically screamed.

"What? What did you see?"

"I don't know but it was evil."

Sammy held his hand around his neck,
suffering the effects of being choked. His uncle
brushed his hand away from covering his
throat. Norman stepped back revealing what
he saw frightened him.

"What?" Sammy asked.

"Your neck has claw imprints around it. You
sure it wasn't an animal or something?"

"No, it wasn't an animal. I don't even think it
was human. It felt like the devil himself. All I
know if this is what the mark brings, I will cut
my shit off myself and be impotent. I never
want to see that thing again."

Sammy got up from the ground. Norman proceeded to the house to check out the bathroom. Following his uncle from behind, admitting he feared going back into the house. Dreading the return to the dwelling, to their surprise the bathroom was untouched. The mirror wasn't broken. Everything was intact. Sammy couldn't explain what had happened. Glancing in the mirror, it all was a mystery to him. Even the red claw marks had disappeared from his neck. Nothing made sense to him.

"Maybe I am losing my mind," Sammy confided.

"No Boy. You aren't. I believe you. Like I said we are going to find the answers. Now come with me. I want to show you something."

Sammy followed his uncle out of the home to the woods. He knew by the direction, they were going to the site of the murder. The churning in his stomach brought on nausea. For the first time since he'd been back to Florida, he thought of going home. He'd not signed up for this shit. All the way there he wanted to turn around, but to what. To go sit in the creepy house alone again. He was starting to act like Hagen. Which reminded him again of the apology he owed his cousin.

They made it to the site with stains of blood that still scattered the sand. The images of the horrific scene placed in his head once again. Norman immediately stopped, pointing at the ground.

"Look at this." His uncle demanded.

Sammy walked towards the area seeing the same pentagram engraved into his penis carved into the ground surrounding the area the men were murdered. The troubled image of his uncle staring at him made him feel anxious again.

"What does this mean?" Sammy asked with intense emotion.

"It means we are in a whole lotta shit if we don't find the answers." Norman conveyed with concern.

"Now let's go." Norman commanded. "Tell no one until we have figured it out. Don't need the sisters making it worse. To be honest, I don't want your Mom, Charlotte, or Lucie to worry. Can you do that?"

Sammy nodded his head agreeing to keep the secret between them. To be honest, it would be hard to explain anyways. How do you tell your Mom some ebony chick marked your junk? Upon returning to the house, Sammy followed Norman to his truck hopping in.

"Where are we going?" Sammy asked slamming the door.

"To go get a spiritual cleansing." Norman responded.

The truck skidding out with Sammy hanging his arm out the truck. Relaxing his head back on the cab, he was relieved his uncle didn't think he was looney. Spiritual cleansing began to sound very appealing to him.

Chapter Twenty

The twitching of her eyelid woke her from the nightmare she'd been having. Rubbing it as she yawned, Beatrice lifted her head up to see the time on the clock that was across the room on the dresser. It indicated the late morning hour of ten o'clock. Feeling like a herd of cattle had ran over her tired body, she laid back resting her arm on her forehead. The tears begin to stream down realizing her nightmare was reality. Her mentor had been viciously killed. The questions of why surrounded her thoughts. The other question of how she would ever sing again without his influence? Wiping her tears, she scooted out of bed. Leaning out her doorway, Beatrice scanned the house to see if anyone was scattering around. Her mother's door was shut, Denise was passed out on the couch. She slanted out more glancing into Hagen's room. The sound of his obnoxious snoring made her wonder how Noah could sleep beside him. "Poor Noah," she whispered before returning to her room. Feeling restless she opened her closet grabbing a pair of jeans and a tee shirt. Fetching her sneakers, she hurried quietly to the bathroom. In a rush to get dressed before anyone woke, she splashed water on her face freshening up. Finishing up pulling her blonde hair up in a ponytail,

Beatrice carefully opened the bathroom door. Scribbling some words down on a piece of paper, she left the note on the kitchen table for her mother to find. She tipped toed through the house until making it to the outside. "Freedom," she murmured trekking down the driveway. The destination in mind was the Pub and Grub. Being unable to call the band last night, she figured she'd just hike there. Some might think it was insensitive, but it was better than sitting in her room crying all day. If she stayed, that is all she'd be doing. At least now she could burn off her frustrations. The walk down the desolate winding dirt road was eerie. The creatures that hid in the woods seemed to be restless as she felt today. Two fidgety squirrels ran by her scuttling up a tree staring down at her. The squawking of the buzzards that flew around the area made her legs move faster. Their circulating reminded her of the terror of the night. She wanted out the of woods. If only for a day, she needed away from it all. The beasts flying above her seemed to be following her. Almost to the end of the road, she saw an El Camino the color of pumpkin spice revving up beside her. Beatrice's tensed shoulders eased seeing the driver, greeting, "I am so glad you are here Scott."

She ran to the side of the car jumping in to join him.

"I just heard on the news. I am so sorry Beatrice. I told my boss I had to leave. Why didn't you call me?" Scott asked with concern.

He leaned over to embrace her. In her agony, her heart fluttered gazing into his chocolate eyes. She planted a passionate kiss on his lips. The tears trickled down her cheeks from the release of no longer having to be strong. Scott always soothed her soul. His hands caressed her face wiping the tears away.

"I'm sorry. Everything happened so fast. One minute I was having a special moment with Denise. Then it all got screwed up. First, I got lost in the woods. It was so weird Scott. Then the blast we saw from our house. The news about Uncle Bobby and Uncle Dan is unbearable. I think I am still in shock." She confided.

Scott held her tight in his arms. She noticed the white stained apron wrapped around him with the silly canoe hat he was wearing.

"What are you wearing?" she asked leaning away from him.

"I was at work when I heard on the radio about your uncles. I told my boss I had to leave. I left in such a rush I forgot to take off this get up."

"You've never wore an apron or that silly hat to bag groceries." She further questioned.

"Oh, well I didn't get a chance to tell you, but I am now an apprentice to the butcher. I am in training to cut meat. I am becoming quite the career man." He announced tipping the end of his pointy hat.

Beatrice laughed for the first time since the tragedy. This was the reason she loved Scott. He had a humorous loving aura about him. She loved the way he could make her laugh by gestures and his analogy of things.

"By the way, where were you walking too?" he asked.

"I am on my way to the Pub and Grub for my audition. Well if anyone is there. I was supposed to call last night. Before you say anything, I know it seems shallow of me to go there after what's happened. I just need to get my mind off things."

Beatrice could feel the weight of Scott's eyes staring at her. Without him saying anything, she knew he disapproved of her wanting to take off. He broke their embrace sitting straight behind the steering wheel. He stroked her hand not saying a word.

"I know. I shouldn't go. I've just got to get away from the house. The woods. Will you take me?" She despairingly asked.

"Does your Momma even know you are going?" Scott questioned.

"No. Momma and everyone are resting. Probably will be for a while."

"I don't know Beatrice. I think you need to be here with your family. If you are just gone, she will worry."

"I left a note." she countered back.

"Oh, well that will make her worry less. Against my better judgement, I will take you. I need to get back to work. When my shift ends, I will pick you up. Just promise me you will call your Momma." He answered with hesitation.

Beatrice turned her hand over joining it with his. Tightening the squeeze, she leaned over kissing him. Smiling at him with her beautiful blue eyes, she whispered. "I promise."

Darting his dark eyebrows down at her, he agreed. "Alright. Now scoot a little and put on the seat belt."

Gliding over, she secured herself in the seat. Scott shifted the gears into drive trailing off towards the city limits. Beatrice took a deep breath driving out of the strangeness of the woods.

***

The El Camino stopped with Scott snarling, "Get out." He leaned over smiling with his lips pooched out wanting a peck. Beatrice threw her arms around his neck playfully smooching all over his face. They shared a laugh together before the seriousness returned to Scott's face.

"Call me if you need me. Or if you should need a ride before four o'clock. Don't hesitate, okay?" He insisted.

"Okay, I will. Don't worry."

"And what are you supposed to do?" he reminded.

"Call my Momma. Can I go now Boss?"

"Yeah. Now really get out." He teased with a smile.

Beatrice kissed him again before exiting the car. She waved as he revved up the car's motor muscles speeding away.

The time was now eleven o'clock. The doors had just opened for the lunch patrons who would be crowding in come the noon hour. Upon entry, there was hardly anyone in the building. The calm before the rush. Seated not far from the stage that lit up on the weekends, sat the band Southern Flare. Alongside with

194

the owners of the restaurant. They glanced up at the entrance doors with the sunlight seeping in. Their mouths dropped open at Beatrice's appearance. A tall but thick man wearing jeans and a cowboy hat greeted her with a hand shake before giving a quick hug.

"Little Bee. We are so saddened by the news of Bobby. What brings you here?" he asked.

"I just needed to get out of the house. The need to be out of nature is overwhelming today. Everyone is in shock or too sad to speak. The surroundings of people is best for me today. To be with the people my uncle respected the most." Beatrice answered with a slight stutter and pause between words.

Hearing the others call the friendly man by the name of Gary, he patted her mid back indicating for them to join the group. Another guy lifted out of his seat. Standing about 6'2, with dark fly back hair. His dreamy blue eyes made her forget all troubles.

"Hi. I am Jesse. The one who called you last night. I am so sorry for your loss. I really didn't expect for you to be here today." He said pulling an available chair for her. Sitting down, the top of her knees trembled. The group made her nervous. Which was rare for Beatrice to be shy around anyone. She'd seen Jesse from afar but never realized how handsome he was up close. He walked around the table offering introductions.

"This is Annie, Gary's wife and co-owner of the place."

Beatrice slightly waved, announcing they knew each other. Jesse continued the introductions of the band, Billy, Terry, and Kyle. Billy the guitar player had long brown hair with a lanky body. He looked like he belonged in *Aerosmith* rather than a county flare band. Terry, the short but hefty one played bass. His afro curly orange hair showed off a feather earring hanging from his right ear. The attempt of accessorizing to make him look cool resulted in him looking nerdier than anything. Then there was the drummer Kyle. The natural blonde's hair stuck straight up in attention. His baby blues made him appear to be mysterious, but his southern drawl gave him away. It revealed the country boy that hid inside of him.

"Like I said, we didn't expect you to be here today. But since you are, do you feel like singing?" Jesse asked.

Before she could speak, Terry interrupted.

"I am sorry about your Uncle, but you look a bit too young. I bet you are not even sixteen yet. Kiddo go back to singing lullabies until you have sprouted some more." He blurted out.

Beatrice shot the now uncool nerd a glare of immediate detest. She didn't need him to point out the obvious. Today wasn't the day to mess with her. The shock started to settle in her heart about Bobby. Without him standing up for her, was this the new reality of how she would be treated. Her stomach began to churn, with tears flowing from her eyes. She didn't know if the tears evolved from her sadness of the loss, or the anger towards this Hairy Terry dude. Whatever it was, she stood up standing her ground with some convincing words.

"I am aware of my age, but you are unaware of my talent. What does my age have to do with it? I have been singing all my life. I assure you, Terry is it? I graduated from lullabies long ago. I don't want anyone's pity concerning my uncle. As Bobby would say, the show must go on. So, you either like me or you don't. I just want a chance. Am I too young for a chance?" she questioned with a strong presence.

197

Everyone at the table was speechless. Through her sorrow, Beatrice's strength radiated. Jesse smiled at his other band mates conveying, "Well guys, she just might be the new energy we need."

Getting up from the table, Jesse announced, "Let's go play for a while."

The band met him on stage. Terry threw the guitar strap around his neck thumping the bass strings attempting to intimidate her. The booming bass would have to sound more demonic than that to scare her off. She strutted her youthful self to the stage grabbing the microphone. Whispering the song in Jesse's ear, he turned to the band conveying what key to play. The music began to play, with Beatrice belting out angelical vocals.

The noon lunch crowd were barreling in by now. Beatrice's voice vibrated all over the restaurant. The crowd surrounded the stage in awe of the collaboration. Finishing the song, Beatrice was honored with another standing ovation to add to the many. Jesse turned to her with his guitar still in hand, yelling over the crowd's cheer, "Welcome to the band." Beatrice fist pumped the air in celebration. Jesse yelled out again, "You know some *Mac*?"

Giving the thumps up, the band fired up the *Fleet* song as Beatrice sang about dreams that were coming true in the moment. All the whilst forgetting about all the troubles she left in the woods, along with also calling her Momma.

***

Scott slung his blood-stained apron in the laundry bin. He hit the locker the job provided for him opening the door, throwing his canoe hat in it. Slamming it shut, it was obvious he was frustrated even irritated. Beatrice's Mom had called tearing him a new asshole. I guess the letter Beatrice wrote was "Bullshit," she stated with some other words full of anger. The mother might have not been directly angry at him, but he had gotten the heat. Clocking out from his shift, he stomped to his car. He couldn't believe Beatrice didn't call. She promised. Promises meant nothing when it involved her singing. The girl he loved lost all sight of everything. If her uncle dying didn't keep her home, nothing would. It made him question her devotion to him. Maybe because he could drive and having a job kept her interested. Beatrice's actions were really starting to piss him off. Slamming the car door, revving up the El Camino he skidded off to go pick up Beatrice. The smell of the burning rubber entered his nostrils. Looking back, he saw the tread marks it had left on the pavement from the angry outburst. He was speeding along to the tunes on the radio when he saw police car flip their red light on, turning around, sounding off the sirens.

It didn't take long for him to realize the cop was after him. Yelling out, "Fuck." He pulled over placing the car in park, turning his tunes down and the engine off.

The officer got out of his car approaching Scott's. Pulling his mirror glass sunshades down, the cop asked, "In a hurry to get somewhere?"

The anger grew to a new level. Beatrice didn't follow up with a promise, her mom's call was not too pleasant, and now this. Why did he even care? It wasn't the first time he'd gotten caught up in the Garret family drama. Losing his mind for a few seconds, the response was of a clever smart ass.

"Nope. Just wanted to get your attention. I felt like having a chat. Where did you buy those cool shades, Officer Poncherello?" He sarcastically asked.

"Son are you looking for trouble?" The officer boldly gestured leaning into Scott's car window.

"Why? You have something in mind?" Scott snarled.

The car door swiftly opened, Scott felt his body being removed from the car. The officer threw him to ground with his hands behind his back. Hearing the cuffs lock, Scott only thought was "Fuck."

Trying to plead his case for smart ass syndrome explaining, "Sorry Sir, I've been having a difficult day."

"Well it just got worse, you are under arrest for unlawful speed, disturbing the peace, and resisting arrest." The office informed.

"Pardon me, but I didn't know I was being arrested. I am shocked as anybody." Scott continued to defy.

201

"Boy, you will remember this day. After a few hours in the slammer, maybe you will acquire some respect for law enforcement."

The officer escorted him to the back of the police car. Before shutting the door, Scott couldn't resist yelling, "Oh wow. I've always wanted to ride in one of these."

The reality hit watching his car being towed away. "This sucks and I'm fucked." He snarled.

Chapter Twenty-One

Lucie ran into the cathedral into the arms of
Father Carson. The agony expressed on her
face told a story of heart break. Red splotches
had formed on her cheeks feeling the horrific
hysteria.

Squeezing his suit so tight, the water from her
eyes drenched the shoulder of his coat. The
Priest's hands graced her face seeing the
tremendous pain. Holding her cheeks asking,
"What is troubling you, Lucie?"

Releasing the hold from the priest, Lucie
glumly looked around at the church. Out of
nowhere she started asking questions about
her mother.

"Momma came to you for help? Didn't she?
You couldn't help her? You probably can't help
me either.

Looking around at the beautiful Cathedral, she
felt the peace of the Almighty's presence.
"This place really is a sanctuary." Came to her
heart while the brain questioned, "Where was
his grace earlier? When Dan needed him?" She
understood why the priest remained behind

the walls of protection. The world was wicked, cruel, and cold.

"I can't take it anymore. It's taken almost everything from me. I must protect Noah. Can we escape here for Holy protection? Can I, Father Carson? She hysterically cried.

The moment was interrupted by the bells that rang automatically every hour. The priest remained standing, giving her space. Lucie sat down on the pew holding her head down. The tears flowed, dropping off her cheeks, trickling down her neck. Taking a deep breath, she began to tell the horrific events of the night.

"Dan is dead. Bobby is dead. Not just dead. Murdered in the most vicious way a human could be tortured. Not only was he killed, he has been disgraced. Sharon thinks our Husbands' are in the closet, but I know this is the work of the coven. I don't know how to begin to fight this." She somberly admitted.

"It took my daughter long ago. I became vulnerable to it with my sin against Tommy. I gave it power. I've lived with that all these years. The question in my head keeps revolving. Why is this happening?"

"Can I not be forgiven for my sin Father? You are the only one I have confessed my darkness too." She whimpered.

"You were forgiven the moment you repented. My child, we will never really know if the poison brought on his death. He has forgiven you, now you must forgive yourself."

"How can you be sure Father. My life reflects no forgiveness." Lucie questioned.

The priest oddly nodded to the ceiling which made her automatically look up seeing nothing was there.

"Let's just say, I was reminded of the very same thing tonight." He confessed.

"I know you can't help me. Momma is proof of that. So, please let me stay here." She pleaded again.

The priest froze needing to take a breath comprehending what she had just revealed to him. Sitting down beside her, holding her close to him, "I will help you. Together we will find a way to fight this evil. But hiding in the sanctuary is not the answer."

"Did you not hear what I just told you? Dan, my husband was murdered. I feel so alone. Momma is gone. Sharon is out of her mind, & Charlotte is in denial. I am alone Father with a son to raise. I must protect him. This is the only place I know to go that is safe."

Feeling empty, the tears flowed. Lucie in a frantic state started repeating the same sentence. "I have no one. I have no one."

Feeling the priest's breath graze her ear, another shock echoed from his soft voice.

"You are not alone. My precious daughter. I love you. You have me."

Their eyes met. Lucie looking deeply into them saw a familiar face. Her own reflected from the priest. She had never noticed it before until now. The similarities in their appearance. Reaching out for his hand, she placed hers on top of his. A perfect match. Staring up at him, she gasped.

"You are my Father? My real Father? Oh my God. Sorry Father, or Dad, I am so confused?"

Looking back at him directly in the face, it all made sense now. Why Daddy always drank, cussing the priest. He must of knew. It made her think of the man differently. Despite biology, he still loved her.

"I have been afraid to tell you all these years. Please forgive me." He pleaded.

It was clear what Father Carson's deep dark sin was now. It was her. He conceived a child with her Mother.

"Is this why you couldn't help Momma. She seduced you? An illegitimate child was conceived? The child is me. You can't forgive yourself for me?" she questioned with waterfalls flowing from her eyes.

Father Carson bent down to the ground kneeling on his knees. He held their familiar hands. Through his hand she could feel his heart rapidly beating.

"No Lucie, you don't understand. I was young and naïve. Maybe not really devoted to him as I thought. Because the moment Lilith stepped into the Cathedral, I was in love. She would keep her distance. I would counsel her from across the pews. One day I insisted she come with me to the alter to pray. She knew, I didn't. I guess thinking she'd be protected in the church, we'd be okay. But that curse runs deep in the veins. The moment I touched her hand I was hypnotized. The guilt that came after was my own. I am a man of God. Why didn't I fight it more? She came to me a few months later telling of the conception. I questioned the paternity until your Daddy confronted me, telling me his secret. He couldn't give Lilith babies. A few months later, Charlotte was born. The man came back in a final attempt to break this horrendous spell. But I came under it once again. You were born after. Not only did I fail your Momma, I failed the man you knew to be your Daddy too."

The information was too much for Lucie. The room started to spin. Her conscious state was fading. Awakening, she was laying in Father Carson's quarters. He was putting cool towels on her forehead when he noticed her eyes were open.

"Oh, thank God you have come back. I was so frightened." he expressed with loving concern.

Lucie tried to get up from the bed. Father Carson urged her to stay laying down until she got some warm broth in the stomach. Suggesting she had cried out all her fluids, he insisted on her drinking some orange juice. He gently lifted her head tipping the cup, so she could drink. The broth he had prepared sat on night stand. He fed the warm soup to her like a baby with a spoon. They spoke of nothing until she drank all the juice and sipped down all the broth. Feeling much better, she scooted up. Father Carson adjusted the feather pillow making sure she was comfortable.

"I am sorry. I scared you." She whispered.

"Don't be sorry. You've had a terrible night." He comforted. "That I just made more complicated."

The circumstance was complicated, but Lucie felt consolation from the confession. She'd always felt so close to Father Carson. Now she knew why, he was her biological Father. Maybe that is why she'd always felt closer to

Charlotte than her other sisters. Charlotte wasn't half a sister, she was her only whole.

"You haven't made it worse. I understand. It's just a reminder of how powerful this evil is against my family. How do I stop it Father?"

Her Father placed his hands on her hands. She saw in his eyes renewed strength, not the often sorrow. She had wondered what caused a man of faith such pain. Now she knew. All those years of being unable to help Lilith. All the years of Charlotte and her visiting, and he not being able to tell them the truth.

"The truth really does set you free. I am no longer afraid. It may kill me, but I will protect you. The question is how we stop it?" he counseled.

Though Lucie's heart was aching, she no longer felt alone.

Chapter Twenty-Two

Madeline woke hearing a lot of hollering coming from the living room. Hearing the heated exchanged between Momma and whoever the poor soul on the receiving end of phone call, she knew her mother wasn't in a good mood. Picking out her own outfit for the day, she noticed Beatrice was already up and apparently gone. Tiding up the room upon her exit, she trekked to the bathroom before anyone especially Momma could notice her. She dressed herself, combing her long blonde hair. Picking out a barrette from the vanity drawer, she pinned some strands to the side of the golden locks. In a rush to get out of the bathroom unnoticed, she regrettably didn't notice the vacuum cleaner cord that was plugged in the hallway socket. She fell bumping her forehead into the corner of the doorway leading to Momma's room. Feeling an instant goose egg forming with oozing blood trickling down the side of her eyebrow, Momma rushed to assist her.

"Madeline, are you okay? Did you not see the cord? Oh Dear, let's get you to my bathroom."

Helping Madeline to her feet, Momma grabbed her arm leading in a rush to the bathroom.

All the commotion must of woke Denise. Madeline saw her peeking in to see what was going on. Her Momma still heated from the earlier conversation wasn't loving like her usually self. Feeling her body being jerked around, Momma spurned out ruff words.

"Turn around and stand still." She ordered while dabbing a cloth on Madeline's head.

Madeline tried to stay still but the wet cloth she had dipped in rubbing alcohol. Burning the wound, Madeline couldn't help squirming. Momma continued to rant, "Stand still." The situation was getting unbearable when Madeline heard the voice of a usual ally.

"Sister, the child did just bump her head. Shouldn't you be a little more gently with her?"

"I am not being rough. Am I being ruff, Maddie?"

In the mood Momma was in, Madeline knew it was in her best interest to say nothing at all. Managing to turn her throbbing head side to side, indicated her answer was no. Momma glared a prissy smile at Denise conveying, "I am not being ruff."

Denise wasn't satisfied with the answers. She whisked the cloth right out of Momma's hand, taking over the care.

"Fine." Momma said in a huff. "Denise, you are so lucky you didn't have children. Because they don't stay sweet like little Maddie. They grow into sneaky, selfish, and back talking teenagers."

"Oh, I think you have a delightful family." Denise assured.

"Yeah I bet that's what you think every time Hagen calls you Lizzy. Delightful, right?"

Witnessing the exchanged between her aunt and mother, Madeline noticed there was something different about Denise. She looked revived. Staring over at her Momma, indicated that she needed some rest or a break from the back talking teenagers. It was obvious the night's events had put Momma over the edge.

"I am sorry Denise. You too, Madeline. It's just Beatrice found a way to get to the Pub and Grub even with all this crazy stuff going on. You would think she would of took some time to grieve her uncles. But no, selfish Bee had to get to that audition." Momma recoiled.

Denise offered Momma a loving hug which she accepted.

"Every soul grieves differently. Don't be so harsh on humming bird. Maybe this is her way of grieving while honoring her uncle. Please promise me you won't scold her? It's a rough time for the family. We must stay united not letting our frustrations tear us apart. I'll take care of Madeline, go get yourself together." Denise insisted.

Madeline felt her Momma's soft hand caress her cheek. She left the room leaving her alone with Denise. Staring into her aunt's face, she figured out what was different about the woman. The fire was gone in her pupils. Love and compassion had put the flames out.

Madeline knew the Angel was responsible for her sudden peace.

Her breath was panting asking, "You saw Sir Michael?"

Denise unsure of how to answer tried to divert the question. Madeline stopped her from nursing wanting an answer that she already knew. She could tell by her aunt's energy the darkness was gone.

"Let's not speak of angels." Denise whispered.

Madeline knew by the way she answered, it was true. Why wouldn't Denise admit it to her? She as usual had so many questions. Only Michael would be able to answer, at least she hoped. Sometimes he skidded around answering her too. Adults and Angels could be so complicated at times.

Denise replaced the stinging alcohol with witch hazel she had put in the medicine cabinet for her own use. She dabbed some on a cotton ball gently messaging it over the wound. The goose egg fully revealed itself along with the color of dark purple and blue surfacing around the wound.

"Witch hazel is much better than this foul alcohol. Heals the wound faster, with less sting." She smiled.

"Thank you, Auntie. Can I go now?" Madeline replied.

"Yes, but if you are going outside, I recommend not climbing trees. At least for today, I wouldn't want you to get dizzy and fall out. Goose eggs can make one quite muzzy."

"What's muzzy."
 "Ya know confused, woozy, just another word for dizzy." She laughed.

"Okie Dokie, Auntie." Madeline shot her thumps up approving of the unfamiliar word for the dictionary in her mind. Muffling her hand around Denise's ear whispering, "The fire has been put out by the angel."

Sharing a smile with her new friend, Madeline skipped out of the bathroom hearing Denise holler, "No skipping today either."

***

The angel waited patiently by the tree for Madeline's arrival. He was concerned feeling her fall. Relief took over seeing it was only a bump and small wound. To say he was concerned about the girl was an understatement. Through the smells of the beautiful nature surrounding the house, he could still smell the stench of Amora's presence. Not only did he have to worry about his wicked brother in hell being after her, the wicked creature was after her as well. The immortality the fallen angel had given her was an atrocious mistake. Not even Lucifer knew of the creature's intentions. Hiding in the comforts of the unsuspecting dark coven, she played them like fools. She evolved from a different kind of evil. He wanted to destroy her. The only one that could, sweet Madeline. She'd have to do it without his help. It was rules such as these he despised. Though he would never question his Father.

The view of Madeline walking towards him took his mind off the mess of the world. It was moments like these he treasured. The reasons his Father loved the humans was clear to him. Though imperfect, they were capable of greatness.

"That's a radiant smile reflecting from your lips, Maiden."

"Yes, Sir Michael it is." The young girls grin grew even brighter with dimples forming on her cheeks.

"I thought we discussed the Sir thing?"

"We did. You started it by calling me maiden. Anyways, I like it." She giggled.

"I can't climb the tree today. I guess we will have to stand or sit on the ground."

"How about yes we can." The angel informed. He graced his hands across Madeline's forehead. The goose egg along with the wound disappeared. Madeline rubbed her forehead feeling it was healed.

"How did you do that?" she excitably asked.

Arching his back, folding his arms together resting them on his chest he looked up in at the sky with a playful thought.

"Because I am an angel. I can do stuff like that." He winked.

Picking up the delicate girl, he flew up to the branch they usually sat. He noticed Madeline's spirit was beautifully bright today. He knew why too. It pained him knowing he had to warn her that all was not right. Hesitating before starting the dreaded conversation, he paused to take in the fresh air the morning brought.

"You look exceptionally happy today." He smiled.

"I am. But you know why. The fire has been put out. I can't see it anymore. You visited my aunt. Thank you, Michael."

The girl gripped her arms around his sides squeezing tight in admiration for saving the aunt. Saving her was a blessing. It would help protect Madeline, but it wouldn't stop Amora's wrath. There would be others to take Denise's place.

"I did speak with her. She is working with our Father now. A great asset to the Kingdom." He softly spoke.

Before he could continue, Madeline interrupted.

"It's over then. If the fire is gone from her eyes, the evil must have left? Right, Michael."

Breaking Madeline's hold from him, bending his head down he admitted, "I wish it was that simple."

"Madeline, listen to me. For every soul gained, another will fall. That is the sad truth. Through anger, heartache, or just dirty greed other souls will succumb. My wishes are to tell you it's over. It's far from it."

He watched the brightness in the girl diminish. It made him ache like the broken hearted humans. It was treacherous watching her sparkle fade.

"I don't want to be special if I am always having to worry." She confided.
"You are special. You don't have to worry. Live your life. Life is beautiful. Enjoy it. Just always look for the fire. You will know by the flaming pupil. Father gave you that ability. Use it. Don't be afraid, it will only make the darkness find you. Strength will keep you

secure, I will keep you safe. I promise you. You trust me?"

Her blue eyes shined like twinkling stars that l lit up the black skies. Trust him? She truly did. Along with a love that would only grow in time. For that he was thankful.

Chapter Twenty-Three

Norman knocked impatiently on the Cathedral door. Turning, looking at Sammy he blurted, "I thought the house of God was always supposed to be open."

Just as the words came out of his mouth, the door opened. Father Carson stood with a surprised face. It reflected his shock of their presence.

"Can I help you?" the priest asked.

"Yes, Pastor you can."

Norman started to say, "Fuck it" and walk away seeing the slight smile come across the man's face. Seeing him turn to leave, the priest corrected his behavior.

"I am sorry. Mr. Garret is it? I have just never been referred to as a pastor. You did not know that. I regret my reaction. Come on into our house of God." He greeted.

Norman and Sammy stepped into the sanctuary of Holiness. The Cathedral was much different than the little country church he sometimes visited. Thinking of Madeline, he knew she would love this place seeing the statue of the angels surround the room.

"Okay Priest," Norman addressed the man.

The man interrupted, "Mr. Garret, please call me Father Carson."

"Sorry Sir. This is new kind of religion for me. To be honest I am not that knowledgeable to my own. But I do know, when you are lost seek him. Lucie comes here. I thought maybe you could help us too." Norman confessed.

"Yes, you actually just missed Lucie. It just dawned on me. Bobby is your brother. Oh, my heart aches for your family. Is there something I can do for you?"

"Yeah explain what the hell is going on." He exclaimed with a sudden obvious fear.

"Other than this tragic event has something else happened?" The Father probed.

"Hell yeah. Sorry Father Carson, I am just on the edge. Strange things are going on. Things I can't explain."

Hearing Sammy's voice jump in, Norman took a seat on the pew. Sammy stutters told how terrified the two were.

"Father along with my step-dad passing, other things happened before we discovered them." Sammy admitted as he chewed nervously on his nails, spitting them out from the side of his mouth. Realizing what he'd just did, Sammy put his hands to his side, "Sorry Father, I am skittish too, I guess."

"Sit Son. Tell me of the strange things." The priest comforted.

Norman injected back into the conversation. It was embarrassing admitting this to a holy man, but they needed advice.

"A few weeks ago, I had a fling with a woman. You get my drift? She literally left my house nude which was strange enough. I look down and I have an engraved marking on my junk. I didn't have much time to think about it. It was the night Lilith got into the accident. The explosion took my mind off it. I kept it out of my mind until last night."

Sammy took the conversation from there. Usually Norman didn't like anyone interrupting, but this was an exception. With two telling the same sort of story, maybe the priest wouldn't think they were crazy.

"That's where I come in. I go to Uncle Norman's. His son Hagen is freaked out, claiming a woman tried to force herself on him. I teased him all night. We watch a movie and went to bed. Hagen and my cousin Noah who was also there, slept in Hagen's bedroom. I slept on the couch to be awakened by the same woman Hagen described all over me. She was very forceful. I couldn't stop her. Afterwards I have this marking left on me. No amount of soap will wash it off, trust me I have tried." Sammy confided.

Norman could tell by the facial expression on the priest, he knew exactly what they were dealing with. He didn't know if the priest's reaction was one of relief that he believed them, or one of fear. Breathing deep he asked, "Is there anything true to this curse Lucie is always babbling about. When I found my brother and Dan last night. This mark was on them. In the same place as mine. Should I be afraid?"

The words Norman dreaded to hear echoed out of the priest's mouth.

"Yes, you should take this seriously. After talking to Lucie, I believe evil is after you. You have been marked now. I don't know how to help you other than prayer. There is not a ritual cure I know for this. It's not possession. It's marking. Only you can fight the attack through strength and faith. Keep yourself prayed up. Maybe if you search, you can find a way to stop it." The priest informed.

"What does being marked mean?" Sammy hastily asked.

Norman knew what it meant. He didn't want it said out loud. Life just became million times harder. "Should he even feed into any of this?" he pondered.

Sammy wouldn't stop asking until the priest finally spoke again.

"You have been marked, Son."

"Marked for what?" Sammy questioned.

"The darkness. Death." The priest solemnly admitted.

"Then stop it Father." Sammy pleaded.

"I can't. It's not like being possessed. I could perform an exorcism. Marking is different. You must kill the one who placed the marking upon you. I have tried before. I don't have a clue how to stop it."

Norman stood up from the pew nudging Sammy by the arm.

"Let's go. I have heard enough." Norman announced.

Opening the door to leave, Norman felt Father Carson grab his arm.

"Help protect Charlotte. Make her believe."

"I am not even sure I believe this shit myself." Norman replied slamming the door.

Sammy got into the truck looking pale white. Norman thought this pastor, priest, whatever the hell he was would help them. Hell, he didn't even pray for them. Then again, after the announcement he didn't give the man much time too.

Cranking up the truck, the two didn't speak. Until Sammy blurted out, "Take me home please, Uncle Norman. I just wanna go home. I need to check on my Momma."

Norman made the turn to his brother's residence. It would be strange going there without seeing Bobby. The realization was starting to surface. Bobby was never coming back. He wanted to kill the person who had done this to him. The urge to believe it was a person not a curse consumed his thoughts. He couldn't go around being weak and scared. It would drive him crazy. Looking over at Sammy, he was already there. Turning into his brother's home, Sammy opened the door to get out, but Norman stopped him yelling, "Wait."

"Sammy last night freaked us all out. I can't explain the woman. But that happen to me weeks ago. I have been fine. Nothing strange until tonight happened. What I am trying to say, don't buy into this curse stuff. There are evil people in this world. Bobby and Dan came across one or maybe more last night. My head can comprehend that better than something we can't explain."

"You deal with your way. I will deal with it the best way I know how. But I tell ya what. That bitch comes around me again, I will do what the Father suggested. I will kill her." Sammy blasted.

Sammy got out of the truck banging the door. The words sent chills up Norman's spine.

Chapter Twenty-Four

The time for Scott to arrive had passed hours ago. The sun was setting, Beatrice knew she needed to get home and fast. She hadn't called Momma like she had promised. Feeling she was already gonna feel the wrath, calling now seemed redundant. Why get yelled at twice? She'd just wait for the inevitable when getting home. If she ever made it. It was looking more like Scott was not picking her up. The dark skies setting made her less brave to walk home. In fact, she'd rather sleep at the Pub and Grub than walk in the darkness. That and it would take her at least two hours to walk that far. Beatrice was just about to go into the pub to ask Annie for a ride when the guys from Southern Flare walked outside.

"You still here?" Jesse asked.

"Yeah, I guess my ride isn't coming." She shyly smiled.

"You don't drive?" He asked again.

"Not yet." Beatrice admitted.

The voice of Terry the nerd chimed into the conversation. Beatrice knew this guy didn't accept her with every word that came from his conniving mouth.

"I told ya. The baby isn't even sixteen yet. Really Jesse, you should rethink this crazy decision."

"It would be a crazy decision not to have her in the band. Those vocal cords are amazing. Give it a break, Terry. Do you need a ride home? My car is parked in the back of the lot. C'mon on, I will take you home." Jesse insisted.

Beatrice smiled gesturing she would accept his kindness of a ride home. Walking beside this beautiful man to his car she heard the nerd yell, "Careful jail bait."

"He's a jerk. Don't let him bother you." Jesse commented.

Beatrice had never experienced shyness a day in her life. Around Jesse, she was at a loss of words. He was maybe a little older than her cousin Sammy, but not much. She was guessing nineteen at the most.

"I don't even know what jail bait is." She confessed.

The reply to the comment made Jesse laugh. Putting his arm around her shoulder, she felt electricity ignite down her spine. Why was she reacting this way to him, especially when her heart belonged to Scott? Jesse started to point to his car. The first thought that came to Beatrice's mind, "His car was gorgeous as him."

The Camaro sparked the color of midnight blue underneath the street light it was parked beside. Another thought came to mind that Momma often warned her about, "Never trust a blue eyed man who drives blue cars."

Yet, she still happily got into the car, when Jesse opened the door. The car though a few years old smelled new on the inside. It had black leather seats with a graduation tassel hanging from the rear view mirror. The number seventy eight hung dangled between the silky threads of the tassel. The number confirmed her predicted age of him.

He got in the driver's side with a grin still on his face. Beatrice with an innocent smile asked, "What?"

"You are just so fresh?"

"I don't understand what you mean by that?" she admitted.

"You are new. The world hasn't corrupted you yet." He smiled.

"Yet?" Beatrice asked darting up her eyebrows.

"Yes yet. I would like to tell ya it won't happen. That the world is like looking through rose colored glasses. But it's not. It's nice meeting someone still fresh. Gives me a new perspective."

"I still don't quite understand." She retorted.

"I know ya don't." He grinned cranking up the car.

The stereo started blaring soon as the engine sent it the juice. *Kool and the Gang* were singing about *Ladies Night*. Jesse turned the steering wheel while thumping it to the catchy tune. When the song ended, he turned the volume down on the stereo.

"I don't even know where we are going? Where is your house?" he asked.

"Take seventeen ninety two towards Loughman. I live on the town lines, just a few miles from the county line. I hope it isn't too far."

"Nah, just gives us more time to talk."

The more he talked to her, the tension she felt in his presence subsided. He was easy to talk too, understanding why she needed to sing today. It comforted her. As they approached the hidden dirt road on the left side of the road, she started to point.

"Be careful. It's easy to pass, especially at night." She warned.

Jesse turned into the winding dirt road. The mist hovered over the road. It gave an eerie vibe. Jesse hit his brakes seeing something

234

slither across the sand in the road. He got out yelling, "Snake."

Beatrice stayed in the car as Jesse walked around trying to locate where the reptile had slithered off too. Finally giving up, he got back into the car.

"Why were you looking for the snake?" Beatrice asked curiously.

"I was gonna kill it to get its rattlers. Now that would be cool hanging from my mirror."

"If you say so." She countered back.

"Yeah I do." He laughed.

Jesse looked up suddenly gazing into her eyes. She tried to look away, but the touch of his hand on her cheek shifted their eyes together. The butterflies resurfaced in her tummy. The electricity ignited down her spine again that made her insides twitch. A feeling she hadn't experienced before. His light but stubbly mustache touched her soft lips. He gently kissed her before locking lips with his tongue going down her throat. It made sensations spark throughout her body. She pushed him away from her, even though she wanted more.

"I am sorry. I didn't mean to scare you. I lost myself for a moment. You are just so beautiful." Jesse apologized.

"It's okay." Beatrice timidly answered.

"I'm sorry. It won't happen again." Jesse promised.

Gazing up at him, young Beatrice had no idea her eyes were seducing. She reached out gently rubbing the leg of his jeans.

"Why? I like it." She confessed.

They locked lips again this time Jesse pushing back.

"I need to stop. You are jail bait."

There was that term she didn't understand again being spoken about her.

"What's jail bait?" she asked.

"Jail bait means you are young. I could get myself in a lot of trouble with you." He answered.

He cranked his car up again steering with one hand while his other held her delicate hand. Driving towards her house, she stopped him from pulling into the yard. A scene from Momma would only reveal how young she really was to him. He pulled her closer to him grazing her plump lips admitting, "You are worth the trouble. I decided that the moment you entered the pub."

Breaking the embrace, Beatrice got out of the car. She waved as he drove away. As the car disappeared down the winding road, she whispered to herself, "What am I doing?"

***

The noise of clucky boots resonated off the concrete floor of the dingy isolated cell. A deep voice pierced through the bars announcing, "You are free smart ass."

The round as he was tall guard, clicked the lock with his keys jangling unlocking the cell door. Scott walked alongside the man that had released him from his imprisonment. Walking out of the jail into the station stood a grey haired man with agitation swallowing his face. The man was his father. His father finished signing the release papers barely grunting, "Let's go."

Walking out of the jail, he saw his El Camino parked in front of the jail. His dad threw him the keys to the car.

"I thought they impounded the car?" he curiously asked.

"They did. Trust me I started to leave you in jail and only bail out the car." His father angrily replied.

Having nothing but shame left Scott apologized, "I'm sorry Dad."

"Yeah, I am sure you are. You owe me for this."

"I know. I am grateful. I will pay you back."
He promised.

"Son, what got into you. This is not your
character?"

"Beatrice is what got into me. I let her get
under my skin. She drives me crazy. When it
comes to her, I am like an addict to a drug. It's
good while I am high but coming down hits
me hard."

Scott rubbed his hands through his dark locks.
Things were gonna have to change. This was
his lowest of lows. He didn't need this on his
record.

"I guess court is in my future Dad?"

"No, not this time. I had a talk with the
arresting officer. I paid the fine and the
impound fee. You are a free man. But Son, this
girlfriend of yours, maybe she's not really
meant for you. Find a girl with less problems,
ambition. Beatrice's family has tragedy after
tragedy. Her plans aren't to stay here."

The reality of his father's words rang true to his breaking heart. The only thing he could do was respond with the truth.

"I love her Dad." he said with a sadness in his voice.

"I know, Son." His father replied patting him on the shoulder walking away. "I will see ya at home later. Think about what I said."

His father drove off, as Scott opened the door to the Camino. Cranking up his car, he sped out of the police station. Remembering this was how his day went into the shitter, he let his foot off the pedal driving the normal speed.

Arriving at the Pub and Grub, he saw no trace of Beatrice. He figured she had already left. Deciding to drive out to her house, he needed to know if she made it home safe. Seeing the sight of the dirt road, he turned down the creepy trail to her house with his lights off. After the attack on the phone earlier today with Bee's Mom, he didn't want to draw attention. The thought was to hide in the darkness to see a glance of Beatrice through the windows of her house. Then he would leave. Maybe by the next time he saw the mother, she would be cooled down. It happened once with her, maybe history would repeat itself like it did that one dreadful night.

Parking the car in the hidden trees that camouflaged his presence, he waited to see if Beatrice was home. Hearing voices from inside the house, none sounded like Beatrice's. By the number of cars parked in the yard, he knew the house must be full of commotion with all the family's presence. Something he was not in the mood to be around tonight. Loving Beatrice was easy, dealing with her family and the singing thing was hard. He just wanted a simple life. Beatrice wanted the stars. The heart didn't want to accept what his mind and father was telling him. A few minutes had passed, when he decided to face his fear of the mother. He was about to get out of the car when he saw headlights floating up towards the house. The sporty car parked. He saw heads join at the lips. Then his heart froze before it broke into. Watching Beatrice exit the car made him gasp for air. He stared as she waved bye when the car left.

Quickly getting out of the Camino, he ran towards Beatrice startling her.

"After the day I've had, I find you like this?" he yelled.

"Scott, where you waiting in the woods? What are you doing?" she exclaimed.

"What am I doing? You asked what am I doing? Well let's see. I was waiting to see if you made it home okay."

"You would know that if you had not forgotten about me. "Beatrice sarcastically addressed.

"Yes, you are correct about that. Maybe if you would have called your Momma like I asked you to do, she would not have called my job cussing me out. Then maybe I wouldn't have been speeding to go get you. Then just maybe my darling I wouldn't have gotten stopped by the police ending up in jail. This day I thought couldn't get worse, but it just did finding you locking lips with that guy. What the hell Beatrice?"

"I'm sorry Scott. That's all I can say. I got caught up in the day."

"Caught up in the Day? You got caught up in the day? The day after your family was brutally murdered, you just got caught up?" Scott screamed.

"I so sorry Scott." She cried with tears streaming down her face.

"Me too Beatrice. I am sorry. I think I need to be done." He retorted with an immense pain in his chest. The more his heart pumped, the more he ached.

Beatrice kept screaming, "Don't go Scott. I am sorry."

He kept walking hearing her family scatter out to the yard. Thankfully, he made it to his car before they could stop him. With tears streaming down his face, he sped away saying good bye to the chaos Beatrice had brought to his life.

Chapter Twenty-Five

Sammy came home to an empty house after Norman dropped him off earlier. The attempts to relax had failed. He was too nervous to be calm enough to rest. Though restless he felt paralyzed laying in his bed. There was no solution to get out of the awful mess. Now that blue skies were dimming to darkness, sleeping would be impossible.

Finally deciding to rise out of bed, he traipsed out of the room he'd been staying in since his arrival. Part of him wished he'd never come back to this place. His father had warned the visit would bring nothing but trouble. Trouble he could navigate, but a death mark was too much. How could he find the creature that did this too him? Making his way to the kitchen, Sammy poked his head into the refrigerator door searching for something to eat. Not that he was hungry, but he needed to keep his strength up if he was going to have to fight this evil mark off his soul. He grabbed a beer of Bobby's along with some lunch meat. Popping off the top of the beer bottle, Sammy whispered, "For you Bob." Not bothering to make a sandwich, he rolled up the ham in long curls to eat. Finishing the easy meal, he put the meat back in the fridge, throwing the bottle in the trash. Then opening his mouth blaring out one loud burp. Smelling his bad breath, he went into the bathroom to brush his teeth. Smearing the toothpaste on the brush, he began cleaning his teeth. Bending down to spit, the sink filled with blood from his saliva. Sammy stood up to see his mouth was covered with blood. He started frantically washing his mouth out until the water was clear again. Glancing up to see if he had a cut, the reflection terrified him. There it was again. The dark creature from Norman's standing behind him. The supernatural being grabbed him tearing the side of his face with its claws. Sammy broke away soon realizing the floors were covered in serpents. He dashed for his room with the snakes slithering all around. He could hear the hoofs of the creature coming closer to him. Sitting on his bed with his legs crossed under him, Sammy hid his face in the palm of his hands. Feeling a movement coming closer grazing the side of his neck, he blared out a loud scream.

"Sammy are you okay?" his Momma frantically questioned.

Sammy jerked looking around. The floor had no signs of serpents only his mother glaring at him like he was crazy. Smelling the beer on his breath, his mother started yelling.

"Really? My husband is dead, and you decide to get drunk?"

"I am not drunk, Momma. I am seeing things that aren't here. I can't explain it."

"Oh, I can. Wacky Tobacky. Sammy, I need you. Did you ever once think of me?"

"Mom, I swear I drank one beer. A toast to Bobby. Nothing else. I have been seeing things I can't explain."

"It's called hallucinations." His mother retorted.

She left the room. Scared to be alone, he followed. Watching her suddenly stop at the wall that was covered with pictures of Bobby and her, a deafening scream hurled from her throat.

Sammy ran to her, holding his momma as she cried on his shoulder. His heart broke for her. Seeing her so distraught, he decided not to mention what was going on with Norman and him. He let her cry until she could not cry anymore.

"I hate them all." She blurted out breaking their embrace.

"What?" Sammy asked.

"All them over at Charlotte's tonight. Even the kids." She admitted.

Sammy tried to comfort her once again, but she pushed him away grabbing some whiskey from the liquor cabinet that was usually for entertaining guest. Trying to stop her, she pushed him away with a strange glare in her eyes. It looked like fire. Rubbing his eyes, he looked again. Thankfully it was gone.

"Momma don't do this. Drinking isn't the answer. "Sammy begged.

"Coming from you tonight, isn't that hypocritical? My son who had a drink and so much more in honor of Bobby." She conveyed sarcastically flipping both her index fingers in the air.

"I guess you can't help it. Your Father stood with all those bitches tonight." She blurted out guzzling down the whiskey.

"My Father? Daddy is in Texas."

The blank stare on her face glanced up at him darting her eyebrows, taking another drink she mumbled, "Yeah, he's in Texas."

Scooting her boots off, throwing them to the side she took the bottle of whiskey to the bedroom closing the door. An indication she no longer needed Sammy's consolation.

He nervously sat on the couch wanting to stay clear of his room and bathroom. Ignoring this mark was not a solution for him. Why was he being tortured but Norman wasn't? Was there something about him that made him a target? The sudden music blaring from his mother's room interrupted his thought process. Looking up he noticed Momma had left her keys on the liquor cabinet. He'd left his car at Norman's in all the excitement. Grabbing the keys, he left the house needing to find answers.

Chapter Twenty-Six

Norman was happy to be driving away from his once home. The sisters were at war with each other. Once Beatrice arrived safely home, his presence was no longer needed. Sharon was being ridiculous concerning the funeral arraignments. He couldn't fathom Bobby and Dan not having a double service. They'd been a trio over the years. The last thing he could do for them was honor them together. To think Sharon believed they were lovers dumbfounded him. Realizing the resentment that still lingered in her soul towards him made the guilt arise again. The night had happened more than a decade ago. Why didn't she forgive him? Bobby's death had made it worse. The words she shouted at him, "It should have been you instead," haunted him.

The statement lingered in his mind. He didn't particularly want to go home to be alone. Sammy had saw something in his house. Who knew? It could still be there, hiding, waiting for his return. In an instant, he decided to go see Judy. He liked her in a weird way. The woman made him feel better about himself. He knew he could do better, but she fed his ego. At this point in his life, that was better than the most beautiful woman.

Looking at his watch seeing the time, he figured she'd be home by now from work. Arriving at her residents he guided his truck slowly, dimming his lights. Before he could even turn the engine off, he saw Judy look out the window. Greeting him like a dog meets his master, she stood at his truck window. To be a heavier woman, she was fast. She flung the truck door open with all of her upper body hovering over to comfort him. She hugged him so tight he thought his ribs might be broken. For a moment he thought she was gonna pick him up and carry him inside. The thought made him grin.

"Are you okay, Honey? I have been so worried." She frantically spoke.

She leaned up noticing the stupid grin on his face.

"Why are you grinning?"

"I am just happy to see you. It's been a day. A long day. You are a nice change."

Taking his hand, she dragged him out of the truck insisting he come inside. Just as the first time he had visited, the home was still in disarray. The not so tidy Judy gave him the same stained cup to drink his coffee. The words she spoke gave him the comfort he needed since finding his brother dead. Before he knew it, Judy seized his hand guiding him to the bedroom. Knowing he was about to get some ruff loving, Norman breathed in deeply anticipating the escapade. Pulling him close, his arms automatically wrapped around Judy's thick waist. Rubbing her gargantuan fingers through his thick hair, with a breathy voice she whispered, "Let me make you feel better."

Before he could answer, she was already bending him down unbuckling his belt. Before he knew it, she jerked down his jeans along with his whities pushing him down on her filthy bed. Her lips wrapped around his cock, excessively licking it like an ice cream cone. The licks aroused him, but feeling she needed some coaching on giving blowjobs, he moaned, "Suck it."

Norman watched her big mouth wrap around his cock giving suction like a vacuum cleaner. Desiring more motion, he groaned, "Rub my balls."

He quickly realized the mistake that was when Judy nearly squeezed his gonads to death.

"I said rub, not squeeze." He screamed.

Feeling her hand loosen the hold, she rubbed gently. It was the first gentle act of sex he had experienced from Judy. Still vacuum sucking, with the gentle rubs, Norman exploded in her throat. She gulped the cum down like a Slurpee, licking her lips.

"Oh, you taste so good. You make my pussy so wet." She huffed.

Norman liked the dirty words coming from her mouth. The more she said, "Fuck me" the more aroused his dick became. Judy slammed her thighs on top of Norman. Her chamber was like playing on a slip and slide again. He needed tightness. While she was thrusting and tumbling on top, he slid his finger up her ass. She paused for a moment with shocked stare admitting, "I've never experienced anal before."

Longing for a tighter cover, he asked, "So you are an ass virgin? Give it to me. Let me be the first."

Norman knew the words would speak to her soul that already adored him. Hell, he'd bet she was already in love with him. She lifted herself off his body, standing on all fours with her cheeks hiked up. Which delighted him.

"Fuck my ass. Be the first." She begged.

Norman shot up bouncing right on top of her cheeks. Sliding his cock in, he was in erotic heaven. He paid her back for the testicular twisting, squeezing her rump hard.   It wasn't too long before the juices blew up her ass. It felt so good, the smell afterwards he ignored.

Falling over on her, Norman suggested, "Let's get a shower."

Judy didn't need to take a breather. She jumped right up rushing to the bathroom. After preparing the shower, she asked Norman to come join her. Before getting in the shower, he flipped up the toilet lid relieving himself. Staring at his dick, he saw the marking had turned from the color of black to red. There was no pain, but it was so bright it glowed. Getting into the shower he tried to hide it from Judy turning away from her. He grabbed the soap from the dish, lathering up his jewel to conceal the marking. Judy turned him around so fast he almost lost his balance. They both

started to giggle when she stopped suddenly
with a strange expression on her face.

"Ouch." She yelled.

"What's wrong," Norman asked.

"My ass cheek is burning." She complained.

Norman turned her around with immediate
fear entering his body. A red mark shined from
her buttock. It was the same as his. She kept
questioning him. He lied telling her it was
some kind of bug bite that left a welt. Judy was
so concerned about her welting behind she
never glanced at his penis getting out of the
tub. Norman was glad that she couldn't turn
to see it. Because then he'd be forced to tell her
of the troubles he wanted to escape from. She
handed him a towel from the rack to dry off.
He assumed it was clean, but assuming
anything to be fresh at Judy's was his own
stupidity. The brown towel was sour. It felt
gross and stiff. He managed to dry himself off.
The thought came to mind of this being his
punishment for all the years of abusing
Charlotte. While drying off he remembered
slapping her when finding the towel crooked
on the rack once. Karma had found its way

back to him. Maybe this mark was part of the punishment. But why was Judy now marked? She was innocent in all this. Norman wanted to forget it all for the night. He laid down on the bed with Judy lying beside him. Though they were clean, the sheets smelled of a musk he could not ignore. Not wanting to go home alone, he asked. "You wanna go to my house?"

It took Judy less than five minutes to bolt out of the bed and get ready. Norman's earlier grin returned to his face following her out the house to the truck.

Chapter Twenty-Seven

The house was silent after Sharon had left. Norman followed not long after. Lucie supposed he was sick of all the sisters arguing. She waited in the living room while Charlotte was tucking Beatrice and Madeline in bed. Overhearing Denise's peculiar voice rave how proud she was for Charlotte not being angry at her daughter for skipping out of the house. During the arguing, Lucie couldn't help but notice her bizarre sister stayed clear of it. She kept the children in their rooms away from it. The gesture made Lucie appreciate her for the first time. Noah had been at Charlotte's since his father's passing. Lucie needed her space. She was grateful Charlotte stepped in to take care of her son. Even Denise had assisted. Though she didn't fully trust the strange one, keeping the peace was needed at this time. Oddly it was Sharon acting the fool. Maybe it was shock. Lord knows she felt it first learning of Dan's fate. She was glad having a real father to lean on. Father Carson didn't want her to tell Charlotte right now. The secret was safe, for it was his story to tell. He wanted her to keep Charlotte safe and praying. These days suggesting prayer to her sister might be more difficult. Somewhere along the way, Charlotte leaned less on God. Lucie knew of the danger.

She needed to perform a protection prayer over the house her father had taught her.

Noah entered the room to give her good night hugs. Hagen waited for him in the hall. Lucie hugged her son tight. Looking into his eyes almost made her cry. His eyes were the same as Dan's. She missed her husband so much already. An uncontrollable tear streamed down her face.

"Momma are you okay." Noah asked with caring concern.

"I'm fine. We are gonna be fine. How are you son?"

"I am managing thanks to Hagen. Thanks for letting me stay here for a few days. I can't bear to see the house, looking at the things Dad set on the table or his clothes he left in his room. I just can't right now."

Lucie held her son tight. The tears streaming down his face pulled at her heart strings. Wiping his tears away, she encouraged him to go get some rest. Seeing Hagen being so attentive to her son made her proud. She had come to the family's aide so many times. Never did she think they would have to come to hers.

The boys went on to bed, as Denise and Charlotte entered the room. Charlotte sat beside her, while Denise sat across in the recliner keeping her distance. For a moment, Lucie felt ashamed of her actions toward the sister.

"It's been a long day. I am relieved it's over?" Charlotte said stretching her arms.

"It's never gonna be over." Lucie sadly commented.

"I didn't mean to sound insensitive, Luce. I am so sorry."

"I know Charlotte."

"Do you want to stay tonight? Don't go back home to that empty house like you did last night."

"I didn't go back home." Lucie admitted.

"Where did you go?" Charlotte asked with concern.

"I went to Father Carson. I stayed at the Cathedral."

"Why would you go there? Oh, let me guess. To pray off the curse. Lucie, it's horrible what has happened. I can't fathom how you must feel. I mean I have known the hurt when I thought Norman had killed himself. Or when Wendell killed himself. But when they committed those acts, I was no longer in love with them. With that being said, I know your heart must be broken. I don't believe any curse caused this, nor do I believe Dan and Bobby were homosexual like Sharon believes. I believe a very cruel, mean person did this. My concern is until they catch the person or persons that did this, it could happen again. Everyone should be on guard."

"On guard and praying." Lucie suggested while also questioning. "What do you have against a little prayer?"

"Nothing if it works. It stopped working for me. I believe in God, but he abandoned me when I needed him the most." Charlotte retorted.

"You survived all those horrible things. He hasn't abandoned you. Charlotte you need to protect yourself and the children."

A strange cackle hurled from Charlotte's throat. Her necked cracked as she turned to face Lucie. The fire was ignited in her pupils, while a dark grin possessed her face.

Suddenly Charlotte shook her head coming out of whatever had taken control of her. Gently patting Lucie on the leg, her disposition changed back to the sister she knew.

"I don't want to cause you any more pain. Let's move on from this subject. Stay the night with us. Denise doesn't bite. Come lay down with me."

"I think I am gonna stay up for a while. Go ahead and lay down. You look tired. I will be fine. I am sure if Denise was gonna bite she would have already bitten me."

Charlotte laughed hugging her. Softly kissing her on the cheek, she agreed commenting that exhaustion was possessing her. Leaving the room, she turned around asking, "Are you sure yawl can be civil?"

"Don't worry about us." Denise chimed in. "We are fine."

Lucie nodded her head in agreement. Charlotte left them to go retire for the night.

For a moment it was silent. Lucie was thankful Denise had been helpful but, trusting her was another story. Denise finally broke the ice.

"How are you Lucie? I know our last meeting was not good to say the least."

"I hated you when this first happened. I almost thought you had something to do with it. Maybe you did? Something deep inside has changed you." Lucie admitted.

"I know you did. And yes, I was sent here to disrupt and destroy. But I assure you, I had nothing to do with this." Denise confessed.

The words stung Lucie's already wounded heart. Jumping up, she raised her hand to slap Denise. Her sister's reflexes were stronger than hers stopping the attack. Holding her wrists tight together, Denise suggested she calm down and sit. During the strong hold she had on her, Lucie knew what had changed. The fire in her eyes was gone, removed with peace. Starting to tremble, she didn't understand anything going on anymore. She felt helpless.

Denise loosened the grip on her wrist, replacing the hold with a soft comforting rub.

"I am aware of the pain I helped bring here. I understand if you hate me. I understand if forgiveness can never be given. I was so blind. I turned to the darkness because so many had betrayed me. Yet she betrayed me the most. I thought this mysterious being could love me. She doesn't love, only use. Any soul she can gain control of. I don't say this with disrespect. If you can't forgive me after I ask for forgiveness, it's okay. It's okay because he forgave me. He lifted me out of the darkness into the light. I no longer must fear anything anymore. For he took that too."

Lucie backed away. Two confessions just a few hours apart. The room started to spin again.

She felt Denise guide her to the couch, leaning her head back on a pillow. Hearing her sister's footsteps scuttle around the kitchen, a hand slide behind her neck. Denise lifted her head telling her to sip the cool tea. The tea made her come back to her senses. Thinking about what Denise said there was many questions to ask.

"You mentioned "She"? And "He"? Who forgave you?"

"Long ago, Momma sent me off. It was to a home of a strict, so called Christian woman. This woman hid behind the cross doing horrendous acts. Beating me, giving me to men. When opportunity came, I ran as fast as my body would go into the woods. That's when I met her. The goddess, Amora. She taught me to defend myself. No man would ever be able to forcibly take me again. The magic brought me peace. I found light of the moon in the darkness. I was a fool."

"Okay, let me get this straight. Momma sent you away. I always thought you wanted to go away. Men raped you, and you found sanctuary with a goddess named Amora. Is she the one who really cursed the family?" Lucie asked.

"No, that was our grandmother Salome. I don't really know how they come together." Denise admitted.

"So, who came to you? You said he came and forgave."

"The angel. The Arch Angel Michael came to me the night all this occurred. Amora showed her true colors to me. It wasn't just that. Living here with Charlotte my heart started fluttering. I had never felt compassion, or even love. I was always the odd one out. Daddy never really paid attention to me. Momma resented me. I have felt like a misfit for most of my life. But then he came in my darkest of hours. I pledged my soul to the Father and his army. Because after all I have done, for all that I am, he loves me. He has forgiven me."

Lucie lifted from laying down. Scooting carefully away from Denise. Thinking about their Momma, she had to ask for an answer to the question that stayed with her since Momma had passed.

"Did you kill Momma?"

"To be honest No. It was my intent. Before I could inject the poison, she died. I think now she knew and gave into the darkness, so I couldn't take her life. Before you say anything, I already know. I have to live with that. Yet he still forgave me? I could not betray a love like that. It has brought me peace I can't even explain. No anger, no resentment. I just want to help. To help fight this evil."

"Tonight, did you see the flame in Charlotte's eyes? Does it have her too?" Lucie nervously asked.

"Not yet. Half her heart still believes. It's the sin of stubbornness that keeps her from praying. It does possess her at times. That is why I must stay. I fear for the children, especially Madeline."

The words gave her an unusual calm. Knowing two souls now believed that this evil existed. Father Carson had vowed to help fight. She wanted Charlotte's commitment but instead it came from Denise.

"I can't forgive you today." Lucie responded. "But I know this evil will take advantage of any crack. I will forgive by the dawn of the sun. Only if you show me you are committed. That I can trust you. I need help praying over the house. It will help keep Charlotte and the kids protected. Most of all Madeline."

Before Lucie could tell Denise what she knew, her eyes conveyed knowing how important the child was to the angel.

Together they walked outside, holding hands while circling the home. United they began to pray.

"Father I come to You tonight, bowing underneath the stars that cover the heavens, asking for protection from the evil one. With the blood of Christ, we ask for a seal of protection around the home and family."

The two sisters circled the house, as Amora watched from the misty woods.

Chapter Twenty-Eight

Speeding down the road, Sammy rushed to get to Norman's. He needed to talk to his Uncle. Make the man see this mark was serious. They needed to find a way to destroy the entity that had marked them for life. The thought that maybe their time was running out made him speed faster. Seeing a red flashing light, Sammy knew he had been caught by the sheriff for speeding. A ticket was the last thing he needed. Pulling to the side of the road, he kept his hands on the steering wheel until the officer approached.

"In a hurry to get somewhere?"

"Actually yes. I need to get to my Uncle's house."

"What's so important?" the officer questioned.

"Sir trust me when I say, it's a matter of life and death."

"Well Son, at the rate of speed you were commuting, death was likely. Maybe I should have let you keep going. License and registration." He asked shining his flashlight into the car. Flashing the light from the front to the back of the car the officer asked, "Can you get out of the car."

Sammy looked over his shoulder seeing the empty whiskey bottle in the back of his mother's car. Seeing it brought overwhelming dread to him. Becoming psychic, he could see bars in his near future. He complied with the officer getting out of the car. The office instructed him to stand at the back of the car with his hands on the trunk. Sammy couldn't see the officer once he went back to his own car. By the sounds echoing when the police car door opened, he was guessing the guy had gotten his K-9 out to sniff his car for any illegal substance. Twice tonight he'd be suspected using drugs, when his only crime was drinking one beer along with speeding.

Feeling disgusted in the predicament, Sammy stood in silence. The silence vanished when he felt the jaws of the Rottweiler around his ankles trying to drag him to the ground. Police dogs were usually German Sheppard's. What the hell was this? Looking down trying to gain control of his leg, Sammy saw the eyes of the dog were red. It made him kick even harder. Able to free himself, the cop revealing his demonic face started to beat him with a baton. With all his strength, Sammy fought the officer. In the scuffle, he was able to retrieve the officer's gun. Pointing the gun at the man, before Sammy's eyes the soul of the officer returned to his body. The dog had disappeared. The officer began to reason with him.

"Son, we can talk about this. Put the gun down."

"Back off", Sammy screamed. "Throw me your car keys," he ordered.

The officer threw his keys to him. Sammy took the keys and the gun jumping into his car speeding off. His head was spinning with what had just happened. The officer had no recollection of it. How was Sammy gonna explain this to the authorities?

Turning on to the road that led to Norman's house the fog was so dense it became hard to navigate the car. He could hear scratching on the car's metal. It sounded like claws of a creature. Sammy struggled to stay level headed. The adrenaline rushing through his bloodstream made his heart feel like it was going to explode. Seeing the porch light on at Norman's house gave him small relief. Sammy put the car in park running out of it not bothering to shut the door. Frantically he knocked on the door. The door swung open. The ebony woman stood in front of him. Taunting him, the strains of her hair turned into serpents. The fire ignited in her burning eyes. Reaching for him, Sammy grabbed the gun tucked into his pants. Pointing the trigger, he shot the entity killing it.

Sammy felt a short moment of solace until he heard his uncle scream, "Sammy what have you done?"

Looking closer at the body, he saw a large woman bleeding from the skull with a bullet to her brain. Sammy didn't know this woman, but it wasn't the woman he intended to shoot. His mind broke. Life as he knew it was ruined at the realization of all his crimes. With no other thought seeing no other way out of the situation, Sammy put the gun to his temple. The last thing he heard was Norman yelling "No" before pulling the trigger.

***

The music was blaring as Sharon came out of her subconscious state. She must have passed out from all the whiskey she consumed. Her head was pounding getting out of bed. Walking into the bathroom to grab some aspirin, she called out for Sammy. Looking into his room, he was nowhere to be found. Through the haziness of her drinking binge, she'd remembered putting her keys on the liquor cabinet. The thought came to mind that her son might have taken her car. Looking out the window she yelled, "Shit." Seeing her car was gone.

Sitting at her dining table, she rubbed her temples thinking about the earlier events. The words she had said to Sammy where true. She hated her family. Every single damn one of them. They all treated her like she was crazy for thinking Bobby was having an affair with Dan, even Lucie. That dumb bitch was in denial. The men were found with Bobby's dick up Dan's ass. What more proof did she need. If they found whoever did this, she would thank them. How dare he fuck around on her, with a man was especially enraging. She was done with men. They had caused her nothing but pain since she was a young woman. "Fuck all the testosterone filled bastards." She thought.

The ringing of the telephone took her out of her heated thinking. Answering the phone, she heard a man crying. The man was Norman.

"What's wrong Norman!"

"Something terrible has happened. Sammy came here and killed Judy, then himself. The cops are all over my house and yard. They are coming to get you since he was driving your car."

Sharon could not register what Norman was saying but he continued to rant.

"The cops are saying he was stopped for speeding and fought with an officer taking his gun. He came here then shot Judy. Then himself."

"What are you saying," Sharon screamed.

"Sammy is dead Sharon."

Sharon fell to her knees dropping the phone. The heat of anger turned into rage. Hearing Norman's voice still on the receiver yelling, "Sharon, Sharon, talk to me are you there?"

Sharon hung the phone up screaming to the top of her lungs. She screamed until she was out of breath and hoarse. Filled with grief and rage, she wanted revenge on every soul that had betrayed her.

Chapter Twenty-Nine

The morning dawned with another tragedy being announced to the family. Madeline couldn't listen to anymore. She escaped to the oak tree calling out for the angel.

Hearing his voice whisper, "I am near." She waited for him feeling a peaceful calm replace the anxiety. Standing beside the tree, the sun ignited from the puffy clouds. Michael descending from sky to ground. Madeline didn't say a word. She didn't even greet him with a question. In the silence, the angel draped his mighty wings around her comforting.

Taking her hand, he suggested, "Let's take a walk."

"I can't go far, Momma says it isn't safe."

Madeline watched the angel stare at the house. Seeing Denise standing on the porch, Michael nodded at her. It seemed they were in a secret communication with each other. Madeline felt a strange feeling emerge. It was unsettling. She didn't want to share the angel with anyone.

Though she knew he was there to serve all mankind. "Was this jealousy?" she pondered privately in her head. Michael could read her mind, which sometimes was annoying. He read this thought very quickly. She figured he would be upset with her but instead his beautiful face expressed a sweet smile.

"You will be safe with me. Auntie Denise will keep Momma busy, so don't be worried about being in trouble."

Kneeling before her, placing his hands on her shoulders. Still smiling he began to reassure her.

"Madeline don't be jealous of any communication with auntie. You are right. I am here for all mankind. You are my only best friend. You are very special to me. A creation from Father. Jealously is a dangerous tool only the enemy uses. Remember that always. Promise?"

Madeline greeting the angel with a smile, hugged him tight. The promise was made without any words needed. The feeling secured it. Michael held her hand as they began to walk.

"How did you know I was worried? That's right, you are an angel." Madeline slightly smiled. It was the first time she'd ever asked a question answering it on her own. She wished she could answer all her own questions.

"One day you will, Madeline." The angel spoke.

"Sir Michael, how did you know? Oh yeah, you know my thoughts."

"See you did it again. Answered your own question. One day you will have answers for them all."

"I wish today was the day. My heart hurts Michael."

"I know sweet Madeline. It pains me to feel it. That's why I wanted to take you for a walk. I have a gift for you. Something that will help protect you. I know you will love it."

Wiping the tears from her eyes, she became excited about the gift. The angel and her strolled through the woods when he abruptly stopped. Putting his mighty hand up to his ear asking, "Do you hear that?"

"What?" Madeline curiously asked trying to tune in all the sounds surrounding the woods. Hearing a tiny echo of "meow" coming from the bushes, the angel and her rushed to see. The angel kneeled asking Madeline to close her eyes. So excited, she could feel her knees twitching. Next, he asked her to hold out her hands. Holding both hands out she felt something soft and fluffy placed in her palms. Before opening her eyes, she heard the quaint sound of "meow" once again. The view of a white kitten with sparkling blue eyes was secure in her hands.

"Did you know he was here?" Madeline happily inquired.

"I might have." The angel answered beaming a beautiful smile.

"It's a Persian feline. His given name is Alex. Which has a special meaning in the Greek language. The name translated means Protector of Mankind."

"Kinda like you?" she giggled feeling Alex lick her fingers with his ruff tongue.

"It's my gift to you. Cats have nine lives, so this guy will be with you for a long time."

"What if Momma says no. She is not really cat person." Madeline frowned.

Still kneeling, the angel placed his strong hand on the top of both Madeline's forearms.

"Trust me?"

"Of course, I do. You are my only best friend." She winked.

"Then don't worry. Alex is yours. I had your Auntie Denise help me. Trust me she is not going to mind at all."

"I thought you couldn't interfere with free will?" Madeline questioned.

"I can't but Auntie can." The Angel laughed.

Madeline started to laugh, not sure to why Denise could, and He couldn't. But he'd promised one day she'd have all the answers. She trusted him with all her young heart. Together they emerged from the woods, with Madeline holding her new furry feline.

***

Hagen stared out the window of his room. Hearing the news of Sammy shattered his heart. He'd always wanted a brother. Sammy wasn't a big part of his life, but the times they share the two really got each other. He looked up to Sammy like a brother from another mother. Poor Sammy's life had been complicated since he could remember. Between his parents divorcing, and his Momma leaving him. To being considered the outcast by his own Momma. Hagen didn't know what happened between Aunt Sharon and Momma, but it complicated poor Sammy's life. Even if their time together was short, Hagen was going to miss him.

Feeling a hand resting on his shoulder, Hagen turned thinking it was his Momma, but it was

Noah. Knowing the pain his cousin was already in, this didn't help. Together they stared at nothing gazing out the window. Feeling he needed to say something Hagen broke the silence. His voice was cracking, but he didn't care. Sammy would have teased him about being emotional. He could no longer keep the grief hidden. If the tears flow when he tried to speak, so be it.

"Crazy that all this is happening, I can only imagine how you feel. How ya holding up Noah?"

"I am numb to be honest. I keep wishing it was all a nightmare and I would just wake up."

"Me too." Hagen confided. "I've tried to be strong, but this is too much."

"I agree. Trying to deal with the loss of my Dad and now Sammy. I knew my Dad's funeral was gonna be hard. Having you to lean on, I can express myself. Sammy was the one who could make ya laugh no matter what was going on. Whose gonna make us laugh now?"

Hagen felt a lump forming in his throat. The sensation one experiences before the tears shed. Trying to swallow the lumps, he tried to conceal the tears wiping his eyes. Glancing over at Noah, he didn't look much better himself.

"It's okay to cry." Hagen murmured.

The distress left him when Noah released his tears leaning over onto Hagen's shoulder wailing. It allowed him to release his own pent up grief. Together the two cried their hearts out until Noah began to laugh wiping his eyes. Hagen had heard of this when people are mourning. They go from one emotion to another. His cousin was most definitely experiencing this syndrome of loss. Noah started to laugh so much, he began to hold his sides leaning forward.

"What are laughing at. It's okay to cry." Hagen admitted again but the words only made Noah laugh more. His cousin must have seen Hagen's despair or confusion.

"I am sorry. You know if Sammy came in the room right now, he would be like what is wrong with you sniffling girls."

"That's exactly what he would say." Hagen slightly smiled. "Or he'd come in here and say something like, hey do yawl wear underwear or panties?" He countered back with trickles of water still coming from his eyes.

"Yeah he sure would." Noah agreed. "Hagen, I have to admit something. Ya know the night Sammy and I were teasing you about being a virgin? Well to be honest I am not even into girls much. I know you are supposed to be at our age, but they are just like pals to me. I am not attracted to them like Sammy use to tease. I couldn't admit this to him cause, well you know."

Hagen did know. Sammy would be making homophobic jokes all over the place like he did with Denise. Suddenly he didn't feel like teasing anymore. Maybe the puberty gene hadn't kicked in for Noah yet, but he really didn't know what his cousin was talking about. He had crushes on girls since he was a young boy. Maybe Noah was so consumed with grief he was talking out of his head. Hagen trying to relate to his cousin suggested, "Well maybe you haven't developed the attraction gene yet cuz. It will come."

"That's what Daddy said about baseball. Momma and he loved that I play. I am good at it. I hate it. What is great about baseball anyways?"

"Awe come on dude. You are just down and have every right to be. I don't think you would be good at it if somewhere inside you didn't enjoy the sport. Remember that. Also, you'll never be good as me, but you ain't half bad." Hagen chuckled hoping Noah got his humor. He wasn't Sammy, but he could be funny when needed.

Noah laughed so much he was holding his sides again. Giving Hagen a push on the shoulder, the comment had produced a smile he hadn't seen on the guy's face in days.

"Thanks Hagen. I needed to hear that."

With the mood in the room a little brighter, Hagen suggested, "Hey ya wanna go catch some pitches."

Noah began to laugh.

"I don't have my glove, thank God."

"Well look a here, a small miracle. I have an extra one. You should have known that. Maddie would never let me not have an extra."

"I really do hate baseball." Noah admitted again.

"I know." Hagen grinned, "But it will take your mind off all this."

Noah agreed grabbing the glove hiking ahead of him. Hagen really didn't know how anyone could hate baseball. Making their way to the yard, Hagen threw some pitches at Noah. Noah dropped a few letting the ball roll towards the woods. Hagen wondered where his cousin's mind drifted staring into the woods. Noah slowly walked back throwing the ball. Hagen caught the ball throwing the ball back. It landed on the ground. Noah had gone into his own world asking a strange question.

"You think Denise had anything to do with all this." Noah asked.

"Don't give Lizzy the credit. Yeah, I have to admit weird things have happened, but really it was happening before her arrival. My parents are proof of it. Don't feed into all that curse mumbo jumbo stuff. You have too much to deal with."

"I guess you are right." Noah mumbled.

Hagen started to pitch the ball again. Seeing something crisscross in the woods, he yelled. "What was that?"

Noah now seeing it suggested, "Probably a rabbit."

"That's a big damn rabbit." Hagen retorted. "Maybe a deer or something. Whatever it was, it was fast."

"Let's go back inside. I'm not really into this." Noah complained.

"Okay." Hagen agreed still staring out in the woods. For some reason an uneasiness invaded his body. He shrugged it off following Noah back into the house. Little did Hagen know, another danger had been hiding behind the trees.

Chapter Thirty

Walking into the funeral parlor, Denise's
nerves were on high alert. This place was open
season for Amora's hunting ground. She was
hoping they would choose the church Norman
often donated too, or even the cathedral. The
technicality of the men not being catholic shut
down any service there. Christians were funny
like that, though both churches claimed to be
nonjudgmental, neither would do a service for
the men. The circumstances had brought them
all to the parlor. Father Carson came to offer
prayer over their temples. The gesture
confused her. Their souls were gone? What
would prayer do for them now? There was still
so much for her to learn. She knew everything
about spells, magic, and being connected with
nature. It was a good tool at times too, or
Charlotte would have never let Madeline have
the cat. This religion stuff was so different.
Even the Arch Angel had told her don't feed
into religion so much, only the Father. She had
taken his advice. The angel had also asked her
to keep extra eyes on the family. Grief can
bring loved ones together. Or it allows the
enemy to slither in to prey on broken hearted
souls. There was much lingering sadness
surrounding the building.

Scanning the room, she saw Beatrice sitting with the new guy Jesse. She'd guessed Humming Bird's love for Scott wasn't as strong as she thought. It made Denise sad knowing she was hard on the young woman concerning the relationship. There was so much hope for the young love she didn't mention to Beatrice. The new guy had a fishy energy about him. Which meant possible trouble for Bird. It concerned her immensely. Sitting beside her niece, was Hagen along with Noah next to him. The once troll was stepping up his game taking care of his cousin. All the tricks she'd played on her nephew she now regretted, even if the words he spoke toward her were harsh. Passing her niece and nephew, she winked while deciding where would be the appropriate place to sit. Her eyes focused on the seat behind Lucie. The two had come to a truce. Both knowing the family needed to be protected. Proceeding to the seat she had chosen, she was stopped by Charlotte shifting Madeline's hand from her own to Denise's.

"Can you keep Maddie with you? Norman is fucked up, and I have to keep everything going smoothly. This is usually Lucie's job but under the circumstances, she is fucked up too." She hastily babbled making the exchanged leaving in a rush.

"Sure. Come on Madeline. Let's go mingle before we sit."

"Auntie Denise, why don't I get a pretty nick name like Beatrice?" Madeline curiously asked.

"You have a nickname, it's Maddie."

"Umm so did Bee. You gave her a pretty nickname like Humming Bird. I know I can't sing but still." She pouted. "I am sorry you got stuck with me. Momma wouldn't let me sit with Hagen and Beatrice. She said they are too upset to keep an eye on me. I guess I am a bother to everyone."

Madeline's eyes began to fill with water that dripped down her cheeks. Denise bent down wiping her tears with a tissue. Madeline was right about many things. She was ignored the most. What the girl didn't know, she was very special.

"Mila, you are not a bother. You are precious to so many."

Madeline gave Denise a big hug while asking, "Why did you call me Mila?"

"Well the name Mila in the Spanish language means miracle. You certainly are one." She winked.

Madeline gave her another hug receiving a gentle kiss from the girl's soft lips on her cheek. For the first time, Denise wondered if this was how it felt to be a mother? To have tremendous love for another human being, only desiring to protect them. Maybe that was the meaning of all love.

The moment of tranquility was interrupted with the arrival of Sharon. Everyone was dressed in mourning attire except Sharon. She entered the building delivering hell wearing red high heels. The energy forming around her indicated everyone needed to be cautious. The bright red dress along with the vintage pillbox hat that matched. Diamond sequins flowed down the veil half covering her face with her glossy cherry lips poking out. Denise held Madeline's hand tight with Sharon approaching.

"Well hello Denise. I see you have babysitting duties." Sharon retorted. "Ya know that bitch always calls me a bad mother, yet Lucie and now you always have one of her kids."

"Sharon, stop it. Don't do this here. That's an interesting outfit you are wearing. Are you okay?"

"Am I okay? What kind of fucking question is that? I just lost my son and husband. I am mad as hell. The devil wouldn't even fuck with me."

"Umm, language, I have a child with me. Just a suggestion but maybe Lucie and you can go find comfort with Father Carson."

"Dump the child later, and let's go by the lake to pray like not so long ago." Sharon toning down her voice suggested.

"I can't. Anyways, I am sure the Father's prayers are more meaningful than anything I could do."

"I am sure they are, but I ain't looking for that. Rest in peace? Fuck that." Sharon boasted lighting up a cigarette.

Before Denise could respond Sharon moved quickly on. Sharon strutted to the front where Norman sat by Charlotte. On the other side was Lucie where Sharon's seat was reserved. Denise feeling her dark energy knew she needed to keep an eye on her. Though she didn't want Madeline too close to the potential commotion, the seat behind Lucie was her only option now. This was Amora's hunting grounds. Her sister Sharon would be a perfect target. She needed to stay close. Deciding there was no other choice, she took the seat behind the two sisters. The music began to preside through the speakers in every corner of the parlor. All the mourners took their seats. The sound of sniffles filled the room. Seeing the three coffins made it all real now to Denise. Somehow through all this pain and darkness she'd found the light. A faith like no other. Lucie turning around acknowledging her with a smile confirmed it. As promised, she had forgiven her.

A minister came walking from the back of the parlor stepping up the stairs to the small platform. He placed a black bible with notes of paper on the pulpit. The vision though sorrowful was beautiful. The room was filled with all different sorts of flowers surrounding the caskets releasing a calm fragrance. Though all three had died horrible deaths, the atmosphere was peaceful. The music stopped with the minister addressing the mourners, "Shall we pray."

The man spoke as Denise felt a shift in the energy. The darkness that hovered over Sharon was forming a storm. Before anyone could interject, Hurricane Sharon hit. Standing up, the crazed sister started clapping her hands hysterically cackling. Her sister puffed the cigarette one more time before tossing it on the parlor carpet. Denise was shocked as everyone in the building witnessing her stomping the carpet putting it out. Lucie tried to make her sit down, but she stood demanding her to "Shut the fuck up." Also conveying to the minister, she was taking over. The minister tried to navigate the dramatic scene, but Sharon asked Lucie to scoot over, so he could sit the fuck down beside her. Denise stood up seeing the minister scuttle buttin to sit.

"What are you doing? Stop it." Denise demanded unable to remain quiet.

"Oh, you want me to stop it? My freaky sister. This is hilarious. Self-righteous doesn't look good on you. As I conveyed to the other sister, you can join her. Shut the fuck up."

Denise witnessed Charlotte charge up the stairs to the pulpit only to have the attack turned upon her.

"I was wondering when the perfect one would join me."

"Go sit down. You are in shock. Come sit with me." Charlotte insisted.

"Fuck off Charlotte. You want me to sit with you like we are one big happy family. We are more than you realize."

"Please Sharon, just stop. This is not the time or the place." Charlotte insisted trying to take Sharon's arm to guide her down the stairs.

"Get your damn hands off me. It certainly is the place. The time to say I loved Bobby with all my heart in spite of him cheating on me with Dan. That's why he is dead. I guess when you get caught with your pants down with another man in a small town, they kill you. The man I once loved. I hate him now."

Before she could release anymore words of hatred, a familiar man walked up to the pew.

293

Denise recognizing a face she hadn't seen in a long while. Sharon's ex-husband Hank was just arriving.

Denise scooted Madeline close placing her hands over the girl's ears. It was her attempt to protect her from the wrath upon them.

"Who fucking called you?" Sharon ranted.

"He was my son. I raised him. I have every right to be here." Hank countered back.

"You lost that right the day you fucked my Mother." She screamed.

"If I am so appalling then why did you leave Sammy with me to raise?" Hank screamed back.

Denise predicted the spectacle would only get worse seeing Norman interject.

"Sharon come sit down. Don't do this. If you need to get this out do it in private. Not here. Let's pay our respects."

"Our respects." Sharon cackled while clapping her hands again. "The way you respected Momma too. Yeah, Charlotte that man you sit beside fucked our Momma. I am guessing they always had a good relationship being Norman bought and paid for you. You ever wonder why your wedding night was so miserable? He didn't receive what was promised to him. He just got naïve dumb you. That takes me back to this respect issue we were discussing."

Denise sat in shock. The mourner whispers were getting louder. Norman and Hank both tried to escort Sharon from the pulpit. She screamed, "Take your fucking hands off me."

They had no choice but to step back. Charlotte tried to step in, but Norman stopped her.

"Norman I am respecting you like you respected me long ago. The act conceived our son Samuel also known as Sammy. I took him away from this place. Why the hell did you let him come back Hank? Part of the fault is yours to share with everyone that has failed him."

Denise knew the brutality of words finally got to Charlotte watching her step back away from Sharon and Norman. Waving her hand up,

Charlotte conveyed, "I have heard enough." She stepped down the stairs with the intent to leave the polar.

"Charlotte, sister I am not done." Sharon yelled. "Perfect Charlotte, I gave everything to Momma in spite of what she did. Yet in her final hours she only wanted precious Charlotte. The one who really didn't give a damn about her until a few months before she died. Everyone don't let perfect Charlotte fool you. Isn't that right Lucie?"

Denise had heard enough too. She held Madeline's hand tight to join Charlotte out the door. Sharon wouldn't stop the wrath.

"Leave cowards. Why do you think Lucie hasn't said a damn word Charlotte? Because it's all true."

Sharon backed away from the pulpit stating, "My work here is now done. Carry on."

Denise glared as Sharon paraded by turning towards Charlotte with the burning flame in her eyes, "Just remember I didn't want Sammy a part of this fiasco service. This is on all of you."

The hurricane left the parlor. The damage was catastrophic. Charlotte turned facing Denise with the same fire in her pupils mumbling, "I wanna kill her."

***

Charlotte was thrilled to be back in her own surrounding. Denise was quiet most of the ride along with Madeline. The yard was full of people.

"Damn, I forgot everyone was coming here. Haven't they had enough of the circus? What people will due for free food?"

"I guess not, but it was supposed to be a wake." Denise wearily answered. "I can't believe you let Beatrice and Hagen along with Noah ride with that guy Jesse. You hardly know him."

"I just wanted to leave that damn place. He offered, I accepted. I am drained, Denise. Now all this other added drama. Did you know?"

"No one told me. I just knew from everyone's energy there were many secrets among you."

"You and all that bullshit magic stuff. I am really not in the mood for that or the curse shit, not even prayer." Charlotte huffed.

"Well whether you believe it or not, the atmosphere is still uneasy. I am going to make a plate of food when we get inside and take Madeline away from the chaos. If you need me, we will be by her favorite tree."

"Just as well. Take her new kitten too, it will keep him from being stepped on with all the free food eaters in the house. I don't know why I ever let her have a cat?" Charlotte snipped.

Denise did just as she had stated. Charlotte was secretly happy for the gesture. She was ruff with her sister not appearing grateful. Denise was right, Madeline didn't need to be part of this mess. The cat really didn't bother her other than a sneeze or two. Beatrice and Hagen didn't need to be around the mess either, but unlike Madeline they had company that would keep them away from any further drama.

Charlotte glided through her crowded home finding a quiet space. She just wanted this all to be over. The space wasn't quiet for long when Norman approached her. The forgiveness granted to him had faded away. Lucie not speaking up spoke volumes. There was truth in the wrath of words Sharon had scattered towards them hitting everyone slam in the face.

"I am sorry Sharon did that to you?"

"Sorry for the truth. Don't try to even deny it. Before you even give me any excuses, the peace treaty has been severed. Realizing I still have to co-parent with you I will try to be civil. Just know this, if there wasn't so many witnesses, I would kill you for all you have done to me."

Norman eased away from Charlotte. Her eyes pierced through him with pure hate. Navigating through the crowded house, he left out the door.

Charlotte stared out the window watching him drive away. The thoughts of what she wanted to do to him scared her. If she had a knife, she would stab him. One strike for every painful hurt he bestowed upon her. Feeling a subtle nudge on her arm, glancing up she was relieved it was Ridge. Not caring who saw she collapsed in his arms. Every desire in her wanted to kiss him, but she knew is wasn't possible. He held her as the release of hurt wailed from her eyes. The moment was interrupted with Ridge's wife Caroline's presence. Charlotte and Ridge stepped away from each other. The woman's eyes weren't conveying condolences.

"I knew I'd find you with her. Where else would you be with in a crowded house? Your sister was right ya know. The image you have created is far from the reality of Charlotte Garret. You have ruined my life." Caroline chastised in despair.

"It's true. I guess you don't really care." Caroline cried sadly gazing into her husband's eyes.

Charlotte was relieved this triangle was out. She wanted to be Ridge's woman in public, not in secret. The timing was bad, but she needed him. To her surprise, Ridge's sad eyes locked with Caroline's. She could feel the long-standing love between them. She'd always desired a love like that. Once she thought she had found such love with Owen. He betrayed her, then broke her heart. If she was honest with herself, that is the only thing that led her to Ridge, even Wendell. She had been running from her own heart. Ridge left guiding his sobbing wife through the crowd. Though envious of the love the couple shared, Charlotte appreciated Ridge taking the potential drama out of her home. For today she couldn't take another interrogation. Seeing the them together put a new spin on her perspective. Knowing after today, her life was going to change again.

Chapter Thirty- One

The sky was shining bright blue to be such a sorrowful day. Norman quietly opened the door to the cathedral tiptoeing to sit in the back pew. Not sure what had brought him there other than he didn't feel much like going home. This was the only place where the solitude he needed could be found. Being unwelcomed at Judy's funeral broke his heart. Her family blamed him for the circumstances. It was just the long line of people who hated him. Judy's family, Sharon, even Charlotte now. How could Sharon reveal all those things today? Maybe he was fooling himself thinking if it was out of his mind, nothing could happen. He'd seen Sammy's face before he shot Judy. It wasn't Judy he intended on shooting. It was the entity that marked them both. It made sense. When he realized what he had done, he killed himself.

"I should have listened. I should have admitted there is a curse." Norman thought.

Leaning over in the pew, Norman allowed himself to finally grieve for all he'd lost. Thinking about Sharon's rant, he realized why Sammy and he had always had a connection no matter how much time passed. Sammy was his first born. He was his son. The pain emerged from his stomach to his heart. The more he hurt, the more tears flowed.

"Oh God." He whimpered.

A gentle voice spoke, "Can I sit here?"

Norman looked up wiping his eyes. The priest stood beside the pew. Nodding his head, the man sat next to him.

"I am sorry for your pain. My condolences for so much loss. Can I pray with you?" the priest asked.

Norman was caught off guard by the request. He wasn't a praying man, not like his brother. All that praying hadn't stopped the horrendous act done to Bobby. Yet his aching gut agreed to prayer.

The priest began to pray.

"Lord God, you are attentive to the voice of our pleading. Let us find in your Son comfort in our sadness, certainly in our doubt, and courage to live

through this hour. Make our faith strong through
Christ our Lord.
Amen."

Keeping his eyes closed, Norman felt the pain
in his abdomen subside. The prayer was like
chewing on an antacid. The more he focused
and meditated, the less it burned.

"Thank you, Preacher. I mean Priest. I mean."
Norman mingled his words confused.

Patting him on the leg with a warm smile,
"Father Carson will do." The man suggested.

"I'm not catholic." Norman frowned.

"I know." Father Carson smiled. "But none of
this matters, only the relationship you have
with him."

"I don't think I have one."

"Do you pray?" The priest asked.

"Sometimes."

"Then sometimes you have one. Yet He always has one with you. People often don't remember that." Father Carson sighed.

Norman feeling jittery as a June bug, started flicking his fingers.

"I suppose. Though I am not worthy. I have done so much especially to Charlotte. I deserve no love. Not even from him." Noman admitted.

"God loves. For we are his children. Have you asked for forgiveness?"

"I can't. If I did wouldn't that mean I have to forgive myself? Well I don't. I can't. I wouldn't even know how to start. I bought my wife from a poor family. Her momma pleaded with me to just take her. She probably wouldn't have taken no money had it not been for the drunk she was married too. I couldn't resist the persuasion, the promise. The lust. Then I beat this young girl. I swore I'd never hit a woman seeing my Dad do the same. But there I was punching her for the stupidest shit possible. I felt strong too doing it. She forgave me for that, she will never forgive me for the other."

Norman began to cry not caring another man was present. Even leaning on the priest's shoulder when offered, he had never felt so empty. Letting the pain wail out released all the anxiety. Lifting his head up, Norman wiped his face again confiding, "I feel like a little girl."

"Why? For being human. Forgive yourself Norman." Father Carson advised.

"It's hard to forgive myself with all I did to Charlotte. I guess Sharon suffered too. I never knew I had a son with her until today. Father, I knew she didn't want me, yet I didn't stop. I am a monster. I would kill anyone who did my daughters such a way. Still, I committed the crimes. I swore when I left Mississippi all that anger would stay there. Then I had to go back to marry Charlotte. If I hadn't of done those things to her, my Dad would have beat me. It was expected. I came from a family where my father beat my mother and slept with my sisters. Bobby and I left when our sisters started propositioning us. I swore to myself it would stop when we came back to Florida after we got married. It was just so easy to do. It would have never stopped either. Charlotte changed, I was forced to accept it. Even with Judy I felt superior over her was the attraction.

Now here we are. Judy is dead, and Charlotte has broken our peace treaty. I don't know why I just told you all this." Norman confided.

"Because it needed to come out. Listen, we have all done things we are not proud of. I have been there. Asking for forgiveness when I can't forgive myself. You must my brother in Christ."

"What sin could have you possibly committed? Not enough hail Mary's in a day." Norman grinned while wiping his face with his hands.

"Everyone sins. Even I. I know she would have given her to you. You are right. Not for the reasons you think. To protect her. The drunk you speak of, well I am responsible for every sip he took from the jug. Lilith came here for help. I will admit I loved her from the moment I saw her. I loved and advised her from a distance. When our eyes met, something took over me. It was powerful. Though I wanted too, I couldn't stop. A child was conceived from it. The man came back a few years later begging me to stop the wickedness bestowed upon his wife. I didn't want too. I had already committed the sin of lust resulting a child out of wedlock. He pleaded, and I tried again. Then a second child

came. We all have something. Forgive yourself
Norman."

"Are you trying to tell me Charlotte is your
biological daughter? And Sharon?"

"Yes, but not Sharon. Charlotte and Lucie are
mine. I just told Lucie, Charlotte doesn't know.
Please with all that's happened let's keep it
between us. I don't know who Sharon's father
is, a drifter maybe? Denise was the Doctor's
that tried to help Lilith when she was in the
asylum."

The admissions had Norman's head spinning.
Did he just say Lilith was in an asylum once?
He didn't even want to know why? It must
have been worse than his family secrets. The
truth was surfacing, the curse existed.

"It's real isn't it." He asked with his words
peaking high unable to stop his voice from
sounding shrill.

"Yes. It's very real. We must all unite to try
and stop it. Charlotte has become under the
spell. The only reason it hasn't take full control
of her is because she has the blood of a holy
man in her veins. The prayers have stopped it.

I fear if the power of the curse strengthens, it will take control of Charlotte's mind taking her soul. She is in danger."

"I have been marked Father. How can I stop it?"

"We must find a way to stop the growth of the entity. Destroy it."

The pain in his stomach erupted again sending the hurt throughout his body. The anxiety ignited again. Glaring around at the cathedral he realized why Father Carson and Lucie came here. It was the only safe place. A sanctuary. Afraid to admit it, he was scared.

"I can't do it alone." Norman admitted.

"You don't have too. You have me. There has to be a way. The strength to fight will come from not just protecting Charlotte but Madeline as well."

"What does Maddie have to do with this?"

"A lot. She's a pure soul. Protected by the Arch Angel. Yet even angels can be defeated. The darkness is coming for her from all angles. Through the love of your daughter is where you will find strength and the forgiveness you need to help fight. Can we depend on you?"

Looking around Norman didn't see anyone in the cathedral. Until a shadow appeared behind the wall with Lucie revealing herself.

"Lucie did you hear all that was said?" Norman gasped.

"I did." She said with tears in her eyes. "I forgive you, if you can forgive me?"

"Forgive you for what?"

"For secretly hating you." She expressed with a fluent southern drawl.

"Well you had good reason too." he admitted.

Norman stood up from the pew. Tears swallowed his eyes again, as the two embraced with forgiveness. Father Carson placed his arms around both of them announcing, "We have a chance."

Norman felt strength emerge through his anxiety. Feeling they had a chance too.

Chapter Thirty-Two

Charlotte checked her look in the rear view mirror. Despite lack of sleep, she looked amazing. The long day led into a long night of tossing and turning. Somewhat like her life this early morning. She was going to toss Ridge out of her life, while turning off the treaty with Norman. Things were gonna change today. First by dropping off the vroom car Ridge had lent, then turning in her resignation. Quitting her job was scary. It had been her security for so long. There would be another job out there. At least she kept telling herself that. There was no changing the mind. She'd seen the way Ridge looked at his wife. With all the gazes of passion, he never looked at her the way he did Caroline. Deeply in love. It had to be done. She arrived early so he wouldn't be there to talk her out of it. The plan was to unlock the office, place the car keys and letter on his desk. Then leave the keys to the office in the mailbox mounted on the outside wall. Dash in, dash out was the game plan. Charlotte got out of the car, with pure confidence. At least she presented herself that way. Inside her nerves was on a heightened level. She didn't want to cross paths with Ridge. Fidgeting to get the key to turn the lock, it suddenly released pushing the door open. Walking in the office with her head held high, she felt a sudden low seeing Caroline sitting in the dark room. By the looks of the familiar couch, the woman had slept there overnight.

"Caroline is that you? Why are you here?"

"You have no right to ask me that. I was waiting on Ridge and you." The broken woman sobbed.

"Why would you be waiting on me?"

"God help me for my words. Because bitch, he spent the night with you." She screamed setting up from lying on the couch.

Charlotte ducked from the pillow that was flying towards her head.

"Honey, he didn't stay with me. Last I saw he left with you. Now calm down." Charlotte ordered.

"You want me to calm down as if you care? You don't care about me."

"I do care. He has gazed into my eyes, but yesterday what I saw, well apologizing won't help. But this will."

Charlotte handed Caroline the keys to the car and office, along with the letter.

"What's this?" a confused Caroline murmured.

"My resignation. I can't make up for the pain I've caused you. Saying I am sorry isn't enough. My time is finished here. I am moving on. I don't want your husband."

"Not anymore? What is it not fun anymore since the wife knows?" Caroline chastised now standing on her feet. "You don't get it. What you took from me. He can never be mine again. I don't do the things he desires like you do. My God, you are a selfish bitch. Your sister knows you well."

Caroline lunged forward trying to hit her. Arching her back, Charlotte missed the strikes. Caroline lost herself for a moment with continued lunges, while continuing to miss. Getting a hold of the woman's wrist, Charlotte was able to subdue her.

314

"I thought I loved him, but I don't. Not like that. Ridge thinks he loves me, but he doesn't. He wants you. I saw that yesterday. He wants all of you. Give all of yourself to him. Things will change. I promise."

Caroline stood glaring at her with tears streaming down mixing with the post nasal drip coming from her nose.

"I can't do those things."

"You can by changing some of your ideas and thoughts. Make love to him, really make love. Go places with him alone, no kids or family. Just please him. It will be worth it because he will please you in return. Your marriage will recover from this being secure. You love him. He loves you. I am nobody. After today I will be out of your life. The decision is yours."

The atmosphere in the room changed. Charlotte released her grip on Caroline's hands, holding them instead. Nothing prepared her for what she was about to hear.

"I don't know how to please him like that. The certain things you do, I don't know. If you are truly sorry for the role in my heartache, then

show me. Show me how to do what you do."
Caroline softly spoke in a whisper.

Charlotte was uneasy but also shockingly
aroused by the suggestion. Maybe it was the
unknown thrill. She'd had dreamed about
things like this. Or maybe it was just the
challenge of it all. Then maybe Caroline was
right, she did owe her this. Feeling Caroline
caressing her fingers, she boldly kissed the
woman with all of the passion she possessed.
Charlotte knew by the nervous kiss Caroline
was just as uneasy about it. It made her want
the experience even more. Sticking her tongue
deep down Caroline's throat, she pushed her
back onto the couch. Sliding between her legs,
Charlotte unbuttoned her dress, pulling it off
her shoulders. Releasing her breasts from their
bondage, she gently rubbed them, giving them
licks and soft bites with her teeth. She guided
her panties down her legs licking Caroline's
thighs. Before Charlotte knew it, her mouth
was engulfed in Caroline's mound penetrating
her clit with every lick of her tongue. Watching
the woman arch her back in pleasure, Charlotte
could feel her insides pulsating.

Caroline's legs tightened with sensual pleasure
of feeling her first orgasm. The climax only

made Charlotte suck her mound until she
screamed out with "Oh yes, don't stop."

Pulling Charlotte's face closer to her, she
passionately kissed Charlotte while easing her
fingers up Charlotte's skirt. It felt elegant,
smooth unlike the roughness of a man's
fingers. Sashaying her hips with the
movement Charlotte moaned, "More."
Changing positions ripping off her clothes,
Charlotte was experiencing extreme pleasure
from the mouth of Caroline's luscious lips. So
smooth, not the scruffiness she was use too.
The lick of her tongue made her want more.

"You like it." Caroline whispered.

"Yes, more" Charlotte gasped.

The suction of the woman's mouth made every
pheromone ignite in her body. It didn't take
long before she was squirting a fountain.
Caroline took total control laying her
completely down lifting her leg up as she
mounted their chambers together. The rubbing
sensation made them both flow with gushing
juices.

Charlotte screamed out like she had many of times on the couch. The only difference this time the pleasure was coming from the wife. It made her giggle at the whole scenario. Knowing this was a one time thing, Charlotte didn't want it to stop. She began fingering her, with Caroline returning the favor. Feeling her fingers in and out of her pussy made Charlotte moan in euphoric satisfaction while having yet another blind blowing orgasm.

When it was over, Caroline lifted Charlotte back up. Caressing her face kissing deeply, "I forgive you. I thank you. I will never have any regrets. "she softly whispered.

Smiling, feeling complete, Charlotte got up from the couch leaving to go freshen up in the bathroom. When she returned, Caroline was dressed leaving no evidence in the room of what had just occurred. Picking up the letter that had fell to the floor, she handed it back to Caroline.

"You will give this to the appropriate person I trust." She winked. "It been great spending the morning with you, but I've got to go find a job now."

With her head held high once again, she walked through the office turning back with a satisfied solitude.

"I have no regrets either." She grinned.

Leaving the building ended her short-lived lesbian life. It also ended her relationship with Ridge Lewis.

Chapter Thirty-Three

It was a long hike across town, especially in black high heels. When she left Ridge's office, she really had no plan. The more Charlotte walked, the more she thought before finding a job on foot she'd need to purchase a car. Knowing she would need to be cautious with her money, since she hadn't a clue where she'd be working now. It had to be done, and she wasn't second guessing herself. The sendoff Caroline contributed would be deep inside her mind for the rest of her life. Reminders of the encounter made her grin turning at the corner of the sidewalk to walk down the next block. In front of her was two options she could go to get a ride. There was Lucie's beauty shop and the Ford Place. She started to dart Lucie's way, but figured her sister may not be coming in today. The poor girl was mourning. Charlotte didn't know how to feel about it but sad for her. Lucie didn't deserve it. She had to keep her own feelings in check. Lucie knew all the crap that came from Sharon's mouth was true. Yet she never told her. It made her disappointed thinking their relationship was stronger than that. Stopping for a moment, she pondered should she go into the Ford Place to purchase a car. Owen would be there. Maybe he would pawn her on to another sales guy.

Or refuse to sell her a car. Her heart didn't
know how it would handle the rejection. Still,
she needed a car. After a few moments of
thoughts, she bounced herself over to the lot.
Looking around at the cars displayed outside,
her eye centered on a Bronco. It sat shining
beneath the sun, sparkling shiny red with
white trim along the fenders. It was a bold
pick. After this morning Charlotte was feeling
more daring, to go the extra mile. Discovering
new things. Peeking in the windows, the seats
were black leather. Though it may be hot in the
summer, that fine air conditioner would cool
them off fast. The more she looked, the more
she liked the idea of this vehicle. Hearing the
ring of a bell, she knew a salesman had spotted
her. Whoever was coming out the glass door to
greet her. Glancing over her shoulder, her
biggest fear was coming towards her. It was
Owen. Maybe he didn't realize it was her.
What if he was coming to tell her to get off his
lot?

"This was a mistake," she thought. Leaning
behind the Bronco trying to hide, she heard his
gruff familiar voice call out.

"Stop hiding gal, I saw you eyeing this Bronco.
This may be too hard for you to handle. Can I
show you some other cars?" He chuckled.

Peering up out of hiding, she stood up informing, "Nothing is too hard for me to handle."

"Well this packs a lot of power. It might be too much for your delicate body." Owen grinned.

Sauntering over toward her former lover, she seductively reminded, "I love a lot of packed power. You should know that."

The blush on his face indicated he remembered it well. The expression in his dark eyes told his secret. He missed her too.

"So, Miss Charlotte, are you here to buy or just to admire?" He anxiously asked trying to stay professional.

"Well since I came on foot, I suppose buying is my only option. Affording may be the problem. With my resent resignation, I am currently without a job. I need to stay within my current budget if I am not able to find another job quickly. So, I may be just admiring at the moment, moving on to something I can afford."

"Well if ya have your heart set on this one, I can make you a deal. Why don't you come inside to discuss options in my office?"

Charlotte knew Owen. He wasn't going to waste his time if the buyer really didn't have the collateral to buy. She had some money saved but didn't want to deplete her funds in her current financial situation. She wondered what was going through his brain. Staring into his eyes it was a mystery. Strolling by she grazed her finger down his chest making her intentions clear. Feeling his eyes stare her down, she knew he was still very much mesmerized by her presence. Walking into his office confirmed it, as he glided his hand across her tight skirt copping a feel around her round tush. Before asking her to take a seat. Charlotte noticed the shades were already turned for privacy. It took her back to the first time she had entered the office. She didn't want to get caught up in old feelings that were still very alive.

"Okay, Mr. Taylor I know you don't waste your time discussing a deal that won't go through. You know I have a budget that doesn't cover the Bronco. Unless you have a plan."

Owen began to laugh. The laughter made Charlotte break her seriousness. The laughter reminded her of their time together. It made her realize how much she had missed him.

"I see you can still be icy. Is it getting cold in here?" Owen chuckled. "But seriously, I am so sorry for the loss of Bobby and Dan. Then Sammy was such a tragedy. I mean they all were. I have no words to properly express my sympathies."

"Thank you. I know my family aren't on the top of your list of people, but I do appreciate the gesture."

"Sit down, Charlotte." Owen asked taking a seat at his desk. "Let's get down to business. Personal and Professional. I know why you would feel that way, I am sorry for hurting you. It wasn't my intentions."

"It's in the past. Let it stay there." Charlotte nervously spoke not wanting the feelings to surface again.

"I can't. I need to tell you. I did love you. I still do. I always will." He confessed.

"Like you did my sister? Don't look so shocked. She told me. I know why you moved on, but why the deceit. On what should have been a happy night, turned into such a darkness. It changed me in a way I can't explain. I am forever changed. But it gave me my independence, so I guess it all worked out. Seriously Owen, after yesterday's fiasco, I can't take on another secret if you are trying to reveal one. I've had enough of that shit."

Owen leaned across the desk. The deep glare into her eyes revealed that he still loved her, desired her. It made her look away. She had just gotten rid of a married man, now she was being seduced by another. This was different though. The love she observed between Ridge and Caroline was staring her in the face. The truth was there. He was deeply in love with her. Leaning closer to him, her hands came across the desk caressing his face. They couldn't resist what was between them. Their lips united releasing the passion that had been locked up for years. Breaking the kiss, Owen came around the desk, lifting Charlotte upon it. His hands were up her skirt in no time sliding her panties down. Unzipping the back of her skirt, it wasn't long before it was thrown to the floor. Inserting his fingers up her chamber, she yearned for him to be inside of her. Especially after the seduction this morning. All the groping and licking was amazing, but to be complete she needed his cock inside her. She needed it now.

"Fuck me." She begged.

Owen released his trousers with them and his briefs falling around his knees. His dick was hard as steel. Gripping his hand around her thighs, he ignited her pussy thrusting his sexcalibur deep inside her pulsating chamber. Holding on tight to his ass, she kissed his neck with every forceful thrust given. Climaxing to the highest level to break her scream she bit his neck. He groaned in pleasure. Their breaths were heavy, as she kissed him passionately.

"I've miss you so much." Charlotte admitted.

"I've missed you too. I will never leave you again. I promise." He confessed.

"But what about Macy?"

"What about her. She can never be you."

The words healed her soul. She had her man back. Married or not, it didn't seem to matter. She was savoring the moment.

They helped each other back into their clothes. Fixing, and adjusting shirts and skirts, to helping fix each other's hair in place. Both smiling, in complete joy of reuniting. For the second time today, Charlotte wasn't prepared for what Owen was about to suggest.

Looking on the wall of keys, he grabbed the keys to the Bronco. Placing them into her hands giving them to her.

"It's yours. I will get the title, and everything set. You can drive it home today. My gift to you. No worries. As for a job, our receptionist just retired, we sure could use a pretty replacement with really good pay and pleasurable entitlements." He winked.

"I don't know if I can. You are still with Macy. What would she say?" Charlotte asked.

"I really don't care. Things have been souring between us for a while. I lost you once. I won't again. I will divorce her eventually. I need to speak to my attorney. It may take some time, but we will be together. I promise you. Do you trust me?"

Was she seduced by her own desires, in love, or just plain stupid to get involved with another married man? Charlotte was leaning towards all three. It didn't matter to her. The heart wants what it wants. She would wait as long as she had too. For eventually she would be with the man she truly loved. The only man she loved.

"I trust you," she confessed.

****

Macy stopped at the Haines City Diner grabbing an early brunch for her Husband. Things had been rocky between them lately. Maybe it was the fact she wanted his baby but was barren. Owen didn't desire to have children. At least not with her. The news was not upsetting to him at all. In fact, realizing he did not have to wear a condom anymore had made him nothing but happy. That's when the relations between them ended. The inconsiderate treatment having no compassion for her heartache. Having no sex pushed him

328

away. That's when he started to change towards her. She needed to be intimate with her husband again. Maybe they could get back to way they use to be. The biggest fear was he didn't even want to go back. Things had been so ruff, maybe he just didn't love her anymore. Divorce wasn't an option though. She did love him. Even if she had to keep him through finances. That strategic move was the best thing she did for herself. The day when she convinced him to give half of everything he owned. His business was everything to him. He would never give half of it to her. It was leveraging to keep him. A low move, but in desperation to save her marriage. She was willing to stoop to the disgusting level.

The guy at the counter of the diner yelled, "Order up, Taylor."

Grabbing the bag, the ham and cheese croissants smelled delicious. She was hoping to surprise him with the scrumptious treat. Only the surprise was on her driving into the car lot. She parked in the back not believing what she was seeing. It was Owen opening the door of a Bronco for Charlotte. Suspicions arose seeing him kiss her on the cheek. Macy waited in the car until Charlotte sped away. Climbing out of her car, she rushed to catch Owen. He'd already made it back inside. Upon entering the building, she charged into her husband's office throwing the bag of food on his desk.

"Have a nice morning?" she interrogated.

"I guess so. It's a bit early for lunch don't ya think?" Owen expressed with a muddled voice.

"It called fucking brunch. I was trying to be thoughtful."

"Thank you then?"

Tumbling through her purse she finally found her cigarette case. Flicking it open, she flipped a cigarette to her lips lighting it up with a lighter she had shuffled to find in the messy purse. Owen's expression was more like a clown that had painted on a smile. He was smiling but she knew it was forced. It pissed her off even more.

"You know I don't like you to smoke in here." he conveyed swinging his arms around with that Riddler grin morphed on his face.

"I see Charlotte has brought a new Bronco. I saw her speed out of the lot."

"Yeah, she did. Paid cash for it." His said with that smile growing, annoying her once again.

"It must have made you happy. Enough to kiss her."

"I did kiss her. She paid cash for a car. I would have kissed her feet if need be. Anyways, Charlotte's family has been through so much. I was just comforting her."

Did he just say comfort her? The word made Macy rage inside. For months she had agonized about being unable to conceive. He hadn't comforted her once. She was his wife, yet poor Charlotte needed comforting. This just took the cake. She'd always thought there was something between the two. Though there was no proof.

"Comfort her." She wailed with her eyebrows darting up. "I've needed comfort, but where's the sympathy for your wife?"

"Don't even go there. You are the one who cut me out just because you are barren. Now if you don't have any other purpose for this visit, I need to get back to work."

Macy puffed the rest of her cigarette putting it out on the top of Owen's desk before throwing it in the garbage. This is not the way she intended the brunch to go. It was obvious Owen didn't care.

"Don't you want to eat before I leave?"

"I am not that hungry. Take it home for yourself later."

In frustration she grabbed the bag throwing it away.

"Well I am so glad you could lend a shoulder to her. I am sure she is grateful." Macy uttered with sarcasm.

"I am sure she is. I offered her the receptionist job. She happily excepted it being she just quit her job." He said with an unusual enthusiasm.

"She had a job. Why did she quit?"

"I don't know Macy. She needed a job. I gave her one. Anything else?" he asked with haste.

Feeling so much anger, she grabbed her purse trekking out of the office. Ignoring the calls of Owen telling her to "Come back," she left the place of business.

Driving away, Macy knew she was losing Owen.

Chapter Thirty-Four

The black birds screeching should have made Sharon turn back. The truth was since Bobby's and Sammy's deaths, nothing scared her. In fact, she didn't think she felt anything anymore. All was numb inside her body. Keeping her pace, she moved through the woods that lead her to the lake where his death occurred. She hated him for what he'd done to her life. All the happiness they had in the beginning had been destroyed. She needed to blame someone, so she decided it would be her whole family. She hated them all for just being alive. Reaching the lake, the moon light shimmered off the water. It was a beautiful sight for something so terrible to take place there. Kneeling to her knees, she did not call out to the Savior for comfort. She called for the one she had with Denise not so long ago.

"Goddess of the night, I summon you. Please answer my distress." She chanted.

The lake started to light up, with intense ripples streaming towards the banks. A woman appeared in a black cloak standing before Sharon.

Nothing in the forest scared her, but this. She hadn't really expected anyone to come. Yet there she was, the Goddess of the Night.

"I am the Goddess of the Night. I have come from the summon of you heart from your mouth. Are you ready to commit?"

Sharon stepped away, starting to shake. The woman glided closer with her every step. Stopping, Sharon watched as the ebony woman pulled the hood of her cloak down. Her black curly soft hair laid flowing across her shoulders. She was absolutely stunning. Sharon felt strange. For she was instantly attracted to the woman.

"Are you ready to commit?" she asked again.

"Commit to what?" Sharon nervously questioned.

"Commit to me." She said with an agitation.

"What does that mean?"

"It means I can give you everything you desire. The revenge you seek, while promising you a seat on the throne I intend to sit."

"How do you know I want revenge." Sharon asked looking into her gold honey eyes.

"Because I know." The Goddess screamed.

"I do, just as my sister did." Sharon confessed.

The Goddess's eyes turned from honey to green. Then they shined red. Sharon knew the Goddess she had summoned was evil, seeking a vengeance.

"Your sister betrayed me. I want to kill her. Yet I cannot."

"Why do you want to kill her? I thought she worshiped you. She taught me about you."

The more questions Sharon threw her way, the lower the woman's voice became.

"I can't because she is protected by the highest of powers. But I can help you with the revenge you seek. I can curse them all, killing them one by one."

"You can kill them without me going to prison?"

"Don't be so fickle, commit to me and they are all gone."

Staring out over the water, seeing the moon hover over it was clear to Sharon what she wanted. Death eventually, but more so she wanted them to suffer.

"Killing them is easy, I'd rather have them suffer." she smiled wickedly. "I will commit, but I need confirmation that they will suffer."

The Goddess waved her arms around chanting to the dark skies. With every chant she would shout out their names with Norman being the first, followed by Charlotte, Beatrice, Hagen, Lucie, Noah, along with Hank. Sharon immediately noticed Madeline's name not being mentioned. Though the child was too young to have done anything to her, she was the child of that sister which meant the child was her enemy.

"I like how you think. The child is the key to my empowerment. I need her soul. It won't be easy, for she is protected by the highest of power. If we can defeat him, we can kill her. Then you have earned the seat next to me."

"Once it's done, I don't care what happens to me."

A devious laughter cackled from the Goddess's throat, "Oh but you will. In the end they all do. Now do you commit?"

With no reflecting or second guesses she agreed. Pulling off her clothes as the Goddess commanded, she stood before her naked.

"Naked is the body, naked is the soul. Your naked body I now receive." The Goddess ordered.

Coming closer she leaned beside her ear whispering, "Your body belongs to me now. Address me by Amora."

"Yes Goddess, I mean Amora."

"Bow to me." Amora instructed.

Sharon shaking kneeled to her knees. Amora bent her over injecting her fingers up her anus. Immediately screaming out, Sharon felt the stir of the fingers go deeper. The sensation of soft lips sucking her clit made her huff for air. A tongue then followed up her chamber. Glancing between her legs, the disturbing image of Amora's tongue resembled a long snake sliding inside of Sharon's mound. Her insides pulsated from the fangs biting with the excruciating pressure of the Goddess's fingers inside her ass. It was a tormenting pleasure that eventually made her climax. Amora came up licking her lips. The Goddess then commanded her to stand before her again. Still licking her lips, she began to caress Sharon's breast. Sharon arched back with feeling pleasure but also fear. The touch of the woman was powerful and euphoric. She was unimaginably wicked, evil in the flesh. One touch and Sharon was hooked like an addict on heroin. The poison of her could kill, yet she desired the power. The Goddess was pleased.

"Now that you have committed you must do whatever I say. Love no one, for love will get in the way of the mission."

Looking down Sharon saw a tattoo of a curled diamond back snake with red eyes marked on her lower left hip. There was no going back now, and she didn't care. Whatever the mission, she would serve.

The silence during the ritual ended. Fire lit up around the lake, with the black birds screeching in celebration. The moon turned red, as Amora held her hand out.

"Sit scriptor lusibus," She chanted.

Sharon didn't know how she knew, but as instructed she danced under the red moon with the Goddess.

The End

Bio

From the heart of Florida, Nikole Rose grew up in the woods. Living in a house of many strange occurrences, her interests in the paranormal evolved. Being isolated from neighbors, grew the imagination of a young girl. The imagination turned into the love of books that she shared with her mother. The love of books evolved into an interest of writing. Nikole's early first short stories were only shared with her beloved mother. Her mother encouraged her to write. Becoming a mom put her ambitions of writing on hold. Nicole lived her life like everyone else until the birth of her son. With a diagnosis of autism, Nikole was forced to quit her job in the world of retail to stay home raising her child. Between the therapy sessions, she began to read again. The reading renewed her passion for writing. Soon after her son started school, she found the time to write while pursuing her once dream.

Nikole resides still in Florida enjoying a simple life with her husband and son. She has two adult daughters from a previous marriage.